UMBOI

ISLAND

CREATURE X MYSTERIES

Roanoke Ridge
Lake Crescent
Umboi Island

J.J. DUPUIS

UMBOI

ISLAND

A CREATURE X MYSTERY

DUNDURN
PRESS

Publisher and acquiring editor: Scott Fraser | Editor: Allison Hirst
Cover designer: Laura Boyle | Cover image: istock.com/dan_prat

Library and Archives Canada Cataloguing in Publication

Title: Umboi Island / J.J. Dupuis.
Names: Dupuis, J. J., 1983- author.
Description: Series statement: A creature X mystery
Identifiers: Canadiana (print) 20210357290 | Canadiana (ebook) 20210357304 | ISBN 9781459746510 (softcover) | ISBN 9781459746527 (PDF) | ISBN 9781459746534 (EPUB)
Classification: LCC PS8607.U675 U43 2022 | DDC C813/.6—dc23

We acknowledge the support of the Canada Council for the Arts and the Ontario Arts Council for our publishing program. We also acknowledge the financial support of the Government of Ontario, through the Ontario Book Publishing Tax Credit and Ontario Creates, and the Government of Canada.

Care has been taken to trace the ownership of copyright material used in this book. The author and the publisher welcome any information enabling them to rectify any references or credits in subsequent editions.

The publisher is not responsible for websites or their content unless they are owned by the publisher.

Printed and bound in Canada.

Dundurn Press
1382 Queen Street East
Toronto, Ontario, Canada M4L 1C9
dundurn.com, @dundurnpress

Through a land of trouble and anguish, from when came the young and old lion, the viper and the fiery flying serpent, they will carry their riches upon the shoulders of young donkeys, and their treasures on the humps of camels, to a people who shall not profit.

— Isaiah 30:6, New King James Version

PROLOGUE

WE CAME TO UMBOI ISLAND IN SEARCH OF a lost world. Some might call it a romantic idea, others post-colonial, but the notion that the jungles of Africa or Asia hide prehistoric wonders has persisted in Western culture for as long as European sailors, explorers, and colonizers have travelled to distant lands and come back with incredible and wondrous tales. We didn't expect to find one, of course, but the idea of a wilderness untouched for millions of years is one so persistent in the world of cryptozoology that we knew it needed to be "explored."

We'd yet to spot any "living fossils" as I led the team up the trail back toward our camp, but something bizarre and glowing had risen through the trees and disappeared into the night sky, into the unfamiliar constellations revealed by the absence of ambient light. There was a break in the forest canopy where at daybreak I could watch the sun climb up over the edge of the world. Great frigatebirds, barely visible in the distance, broke formation as they skimmed the water looking for prey. The volcano toward the centre of the island could be clearly seen in the distance, a collar of greenery rising around its neck. With the ocean at our backs we continued toward camp, the volcano standing ominously to the right. It was more of a mountain, actually, since it hadn't erupted for eleven thousand years, but that was cold comfort.

"Does it bother you, Laura?" Saad asked as he sidled up next to me.

I'd told him once about my fear of volcanoes, but he'd never brought it up. Growing up near Mount St. Helens, volcanic eruptions for me were not a remote threat but a real possibility. I had always pictured our town as the next Pompeii, our bodies preserved for the ages in walls of ash.

"I'm fine," I said, hooking my thumbs under the straps of my backpack. "What are the chances it would become active now?"

"Slim to none," he said, giving me one of his rare smiles.

The trail widened as we approached the clearing where we'd set up camp. Our team had spent the night hunting an extant pterosaur that glowed in the dark, known as the "Ropen." Its name meant "demon flyer" and it supposedly flew above the canopy at night on leathery wings, emitting a haunting bioluminescent glow.

Rumoured to be a nocturnal creature, we stalked the jungle at night looking for evidence of the Ropen's existence. While the team of British researchers from NatureWorld's U.K. affiliate were training their night-vision cameras on the trees and the forest floor, we tilted ours upward. Chris, our cameraman, was enjoying the toys he got to play with, the drones and the camera traps, and the rest of us were happy to take part in a legitimate expedition. Well, maybe Danny, the producer, and the new guy, Joshua, weren't enjoying themselves, but I couldn't care less.

"I've never looked more forward to a cot in my life," Danny announced, veering toward the large tent where the men slept. "I'll say this for you, Laura, at least you picked a tropical location this time. I was getting pale as a ghost."

The men were eager to dump their packs in the tent and either sleep or head to the commissary for something to eat. The straps of my pack had made permanent tracks around my shoulders and I wanted nothing more than to take it off, lay down on my cot, throw something over my face, and drop off to sleep.

Across the camp, I saw Lindsay emerge from the commissary tent and walk toward me. I smiled, relieved she'd made it back safely.

"There you are," I said. "How were the caves?"

"They go deeper than I would have thought," she said. "I'd love to go back with proper gear."

That was the first time she seemed legitimately excited to be on the island.

"There might be time for that," I said. "But I need a little rest before we start shooting again tonight."

"Me, too."

The scientists from the U.K. team were up at dawn, and for the most part stayed up until nightfall, so we expected we'd have the tent to ourselves. We had a few hours before we had to wake up for the night shoot.

I pushed the tent flap aside and walked in, several thoughts competing with the sensations of fatigue for my attention. The first thing I noticed was an odd smell, different from the thick rainforest air. Then the flies. A sense of danger set off alarms in my brain. Then I saw him. I stopped dead in my tracks, gasped, and turned to push Lindsay back out the door. But I was too late. She stood there in the doorway, open-mouthed, looking as if she'd stepped on the third rail of a subway track.

He was lying on Lindsay's cot. On the ground beside him was my monogrammed Remington knife, the compact steel blade stained red with blood. I knew he was dead.

ONE

Standard models of evolution assert that all species of dinosaurs and pterosaurs became extinct long ago and that their fossils are evidence for unlimited common ancestry, the extinction of the vast majority of species opening the way for those more fit to survive. Although all species of pterosaurs could have been destroyed by the Flood and post-Flood changes, the young-earth view holds out the possibility of extant pterosaurs. Investigations of reports of creatures whose descriptions suggest Rhamphorhynchoid pterosaurs in remote areas of Papua New Guinea were carried out between 1994 and 2007.

— Jonathan D. Whitcomb, "Reports of Living Pterosaurs in the Southwest Pacific"

THE WINDOWS IN THE GYM OF THE GRAND Papua Hotel looked out on Ela Beach and Walter Bay. The Pacific Ocean was nothing more than undulating tar; the outline of a palm tree in the foreground gave a sense of dimension. Otherwise, there was nothing in the distant night but water. Queensland was somewhere in that direction, too far to see even if it were daytime.

Saad, Duncan, and I had spent the last twenty minutes on the treadmills, each of us at various intensities, trying to loosen up for what was to come. We all knew we'd have to contend with the jet lag that came with flying from the U.S. to Papua New Guinea. Some of the crew would rely on sleeping pills, others valerian root or chamomile tea. The three of us chose exercise to tire ourselves out.

We had the gym to ourselves. The flat-screen TV mounted on the wall was dark. An Archie Shepp album played on my phone and the belts of the treadmills whirred, masking the laboured breathing of my two colleagues.

I was the first to get off the treadmill, but not because I was tired. "So, are we going to do this, or what?"

Saad knew I was speaking to him. He lowered the intensity on his treadmill so the black conveyer belt whooshed slower and slower until he shut it off completely. "I thought, between the long flight and the jogging, you might let me off the hook."

I walked over to my gym bag and took out a pair of four-ounce, open-fingered gloves and tossed them over to him. While he slid his hands inside and strapped them around his wrists, I took out my focus mitts and put them on.

"Is this —" Duncan started.

"Don't make a *Fight Club* joke," I said, cutting him off.

"Never mind," he said, turning back to his reflection in the window. "You couldn't talk about it even if it were."

I approached Saad, who was getting into his stance. It was like watching a machine start up, all the parts setting themselves, starting with foot placement and continuing up through his torso, his hands finding their place to cover his jawline, ending with the chin tuck. His movements were slow and deliberate enough that I could almost read the checklist in his head as he recalled what I had taught him.

"Start with the jab, cross, elbow, elbow, rear knee?" I asked.

He nodded, looking down at his own body one more time to make sure every part was set in the correct position. I held up my right hand, gloved in the black leather focus mitt with a white circle painted in the palm acting as a bullseye.

"Jab," I said.

He stepped forward with his lead foot, sliding the rear foot after to maintain the same distance between them. He popped a quick jab at the glove, rotating his body and turning his fist over so that the thumb and forefinger faced the floor as the punch connected.

"Good," I said as his left hand retreated to the guard position by his left cheekbone.

His right hand travelled the course the left had set, as he turned on his back foot, rotating at the hips, then the shoulders, delivering a cross that was noticeably better, stronger and faster, than when we'd first started his training upon returning home from Newfoundland. The impact made a pop against my leather mitt before his hand quickly pulled back into a defensive position along his jawline. Saad didn't stop his momentum, turning again with the left side of his body, bringing his elbow up and across on a level trajectory toward the mitt in my left hand.

"Nice," I said.

He pivoted again, like the agitator in a washing machine, bringing his right elbow to strike the mitt. This time, instead of returning to a guard position, he dropped his right hand onto my shoulder, pulling me downward while driving his right knee up into the mitt I had waiting. After landing the last strike he backed off and reset his position.

"Is that Thai boxing?" Duncan asked.

The paleontologist from the University of Southampton powered down his treadmill, released his grip on the handles, and stepped off.

"Sort of," I said, "but repurposed for combatives."

"Like self-defence?" he asked.

"Essentially. Combatives is more a mindset, using moves from martial arts and dirty boxing to stop an attacker. It's more than self-defence because there's a realization that you're not safe so long as your attacker is still standing."

"That sounds violent," Duncan said, putting his hands on his hips. "I'm a black belt in judo."

"Really?" Saad said.

"I did not know that," I added.

"My stepdad was one of those blokes who was mad about Steven Seagal movies back in the eighties. He talked my mom into the whole 'a young boy needs discipline and the martial arts teach discipline' thing. The rest is history. I haven't been to the dojo in ages, though."

My father was never into martial arts movies, as he mainly watched Westerns, but he did like Steven Seagal. But when it came to teaching me to defend myself, there was nothing of an "art" about it, and that mindset still influenced how I trained, even with Muay Thai and self-defence classes.

"Judo is the throwing art," Saad asked, "the one about leverage and submissions, right?"

"Yes," Duncan said, "although some styles incorporate rudimentary striking."

"I'm still in the rudimentary phase," Saad said.

"Your technique looks pretty crisp to me," Duncan said.

"He's a fast learner," I said.

"I've never been athletic, but Laura explains it in a way I understand, step by step while providing the reason behind each movement."

"Can I give it a go?" Duncan asked. "I'll go lighter since I haven't any gloves."

Duncan attempted the same combination from memory, making the mistakes that all beginners make. He didn't twist his hips to generate power, he didn't make sure to bring his hands quickly back to guard his face. It was the slow, concerted effort that came before each technique was burned into the muscle memory.

"Not bad," I said.

"Did I mention judo is more my forte?"

Saad smiled.

"Practice makes perfect," I said. "I'm not really one for throws and foot sweeps."

Duncan looked down at his knuckles, then at the pinkish marks on his elbows.

"I think I'll stick to throws," he said, "not like I ever need to use them."

"Maybe you could show me some basics," Saad said.

"I'd be delighted," Duncan replied. "You don't mind me taking over your lesson, do you, Laura?"

"Be my guest," I said, then turned to Saad. "Remember what I told you, though, anytime someone can grab you, you can and should hit them."

Duncan looked at me with trepidation before moving toward Saad, I think wondering what he was getting himself into. He began demonstrating to him a basic hip throw. I understood the mechanics, but was never comfortable with voluntarily attaching myself to an attacker when I could strike them and keep moving. There are takedowns from the Filipino martial arts that my instructor included in his curriculum that naturally blended with strikes, but the throws that involved me dropping my hands from my jaw were not for me.

"What the hell's going on here?"

Danny was standing in the doorway.

Saad and Duncan, who looked like one was teaching the other how to waltz, stood bolt upright like schoolboys caught stealing answers to an exam.

"Which one of you is trying out for the UFC?" he asked, taking a few steps into the room.

Danny, our producer, was the morning-jog-and-steam-room type. I could picture him on a treadmill as the sun rose over the water, talking to the network on his headset while walking at a brisk pace. He didn't look too delicate for martial arts, but as though the close proximity to another sweaty human it required would be utterly repulsive to him.

"Just exploring our career options," I said. "I mean, how long can we go on searching for cryptids and coming up empty?"

"Is that a rhetorical question? *Finding Bigfoot* was on the air for nine seasons, and still no Bigfoot."

Bigfoot is Bigfoot, I thought, one of the most enduring myths of our time. There will always be shows about it, powered by the limitless desire to believe that something like us, but not us, is just a tree-covered mountain away.

"What's with the music, if I can call it that?" Danny asked, the look on his face reminiscent of someone who was smelling rotten eggs.

"It's free jazz," I said.

"It had better be free. No one would pay money to listen to that," he said, laughing. "You work out to jazz?"

"Only when I'm on a treadmill," I said. "Something my dad taught me. Listen only to one instrument throughout a whole song. Follow it. Once you can do that, it's easy to pick out the sound of one bird or one animal in a forest full of life."

"Most people seem less strange the more you get to know them," Danny said. "In your case, it's the opposite."

I rolled my eyes. "What brings you down here? I thought you'd be cozying up to the minibar then calling it a night."

"My internal clock doesn't know what time it is. I just came to let you know that my pterosaur guy has arrived."

Duncan looked wide-eyed, first at Danny, then at me. I shrugged. It was the first I was hearing of it.

"I thought I was the pterosaur guy?" Duncan said, sounding hurt.

"You're definitely a pterosaur guy, but I brought in another."

"Why don't I like the sound of that?" I asked.

"A plurality of opinions is always better for science ... and for discourse," Danny said.

Duncan and I looked at each other.

"And ratings," I heard Saad say under his breath.

My skin, which had been warm with sweat, now felt cold and clammy — part spider-sense, part BS-detector.

"Why do I get the feeling that this other 'expert' is no expert at all?" I asked.

"He is a credentialed paleontologist, with a Ph.D. from the University of Rhode Island."

"Oh, Danny, you didn't ..." Duncan said, his mouth slightly agape.

Danny didn't turn to face me, but his eyes slid over to gauge my reaction. I put out an order to my face to stop all involuntary twitches, expressions, or telling glances. With the gag order in place, Danny's eyes got nothing and returned to Duncan.

"He happened to be in Papua New Guinea, so I thought I'd ask if he wanted to come to Umboi with us."

The "he" in question was Dr. Joshua Brooks, a man who paradoxically held degrees in geology and paleontology while holding young-earth creationist beliefs. Somehow, he managed to write his dissertation on the population distribution of Azhdarchid pterosaurs, which lived mostly during the late Cretaceous period, which ended sixty-five million years ago, while believing in his heart of hearts that the earth was only ten thousand years old.

"He's just getting settled in, then he's meeting me in the bar. I thought you might want to come up and say hi."

I glanced up at the clock on the wall. "Sure, I'll say hi, once I grab a shower and clean up a little."

"Great," he said. "Have you seen Lindsay, by the way?"

"Not since we got here. She went straight to her room and hasn't come out since."

"It was a long flight, and it's her last chance to sleep in a bed for five days, so I guess we can leave her out of this one," Danny said.

"That's downright human of you," I said.

He brought his index finger up to his lips. "Don't tell anyone," he whispered.

He turned and left, and it was as if he'd taken all the words with him. Duncan, Saad, and I just stood there, three points of a scalene triangle, grasping for thoughts that dispersed like a morning fog.

"Well …" Duncan said finally. "I suppose that concludes the martial arts lesson." He slapped his hands down on his navy-blue pant legs and gave a half bow.

"I don't understand," Saad said, "did we agree to talk about creationism on our science show?"

"No," I said. "*We* didn't decide anything."

Danny was nowhere in sight when we came out of the gym. We rode the elevator to the seventh floor, the last of the Grand Papua's so-called "Premier Floors," and walked down the hall with counterfeit nonchalance. I for one wanted to beat the others to the bar for a chance to speak to Danny before Brooks or the others came.

Setting a record time for showering, I tied my hair back and threw on a clean T-shirt and jeans before leaving my room and heading down the hall. I paused at Saad's door, listening, but I could hear no movement inside. Outside Duncan's door I could hear the British paleontologist's voice, the pitch higher than usual, his tone more playful. He was clearly on the phone with his family, talking to either his two-year-old son or four-year-old daughter. I passed Lindsay's door and I thought about knocking to see if she'd like to grab a drink, but her mood since we touched down had been sombre bordering on melancholic. If I were in her place, would I want someone to check in on me, or would I prefer time alone? If it was a friend, sure, I'd like a knock on the door. But I can't even tell if Lindsay and I are friends, or just co-workers.

I walked by Chris's door without stopping. Our cameraman was thick as thieves with Danny. No doubt he already knew the plan and would be down in the bar if he wanted to be.

Downstairs I found Danny perched on a leather stool at the corner of the marble bar, a tumbler of Scotch in his hand and his jacket open, his other hand in his pocket. He looked like he was modeling for a cologne ad in a men's magazine. The bar was empty aside from him and the bartender. She was a tall woman with long black hair tied back in a ponytail. Her eyes were shaped like a cat's and she had the cheekbones to match, her skin unnaturally bronzed and free of blemishes.

The ocean breeze rolled through the open wood shutters, the whitecaps of the waves visible through the slats as they crashed against the beach. Danny noticed me and raised his glass before sliding off the stool and heading toward one of the circular tables near the window.

"I knew you'd be the first one down," he said.

The Grand Bar felt very much of the past, a throwback to some Victorian club where gentlemen drank and played chess away from the womenfolk. Were it not for the palm trees, we might have been in London. There was also something anachronistic in how the bartender stood at attention, not speaking but ready to receive my order.

"Tonic water, please."

She gave me a slight smile and reached under the bar for a glass.

"That's almost like saying 'I knew you'd come running out' after setting fire to my house," I said to Danny from the bar.

"I'm surprised burning houses is not a touchy subject for you," he said, referring to the time Saad and I were caught inside a burning house that belonged to a notorious Bigfoot hoaxer.

"I didn't even think of that," I said. "But let's stay on topic, shall we? You knew I'd hurry down to ask you what the hell you're doing?"

"I thought we'd reached an understanding, in Newfoundland. I'll do what's necessary to make *Creature X* successful, and you and your team prove how the scientific method works."

"This sounds like we're 'teaching the controversy' or however anti-science interests try to push their narrative into the conversation."

"Not at all," Danny said. "You'll have ample opportunity to prove why the scientific consensus is correct."

The bartender laid a cocktail napkin with the words *Grand Papua* written across the white surface in gold letters on the bar, placed my glass on top, then slid them across the marble bar.

"Thank you." I walked over to the table and sat down in one of the yellow leather tub chairs. "Contrary to popular belief," I said, "I'm not out to challenge any person's religious views. But we agreed that we were doing a science show about cryptids."

"And Dr. Brooks is a respected scientist," Danny said. "Believe me, I could've had any number of kooks on the show. Audiences and the network would love it." He took a long sip of scotch and paused, savouring it. "What are you worried about, Laura? You'll still get your say when it comes to the editing. I won't cut the episode in a way that lends Dr. Brooks equal credibility to Dr. Laidlaw or the scientific consensus." He raised his eyebrows as if to say "so there."

"Don't you think giving creationism another platform seriously undermines what we're trying to accomplish? It's bad enough intelligent design is still getting snuck into textbooks stateside."

"What I'm trying to accomplish is creating a show that is popular enough and lasts long enough that you can get your message out there. There'll be no platform at all if the network pulls the show. It's hard enough to keep cable networks viable with streaming platforms so appealing to younger demographics. Plus, we've gotta contend with reboots of old classics like *In Search of …* and *Unsolved Mysteries*. This is a business after all."

He paused again, sipping his drink and looking over the rim of his glass toward the doorway. "Are you afraid of how it will look in front of the other team? Is that it? Are you concerned those British biologists will think you're a joke? They probably already do, no offence. We are doing a show about monsters, for god's sake."

NatureWorld's U.K. counterpart was currently filming an episode of their program *Explorer* on Umboi Island. They'd be there for another three days, during which time we'd be sharing a campsite and certain equipment. We'd be out chasing glow-in-the-dark living pterosaurs while they hoped to catalogue novel species of butterflies, birds, and perhaps even small- to medium-sized mammals.

"We're doing a show about science," I said, "first and foremost."

Danny looked over my shoulder and stood up. I turned to see a man walk into the bar. He was well coiffed and dressed in business casual, but nothing particularly stylish. His grey-flecked brown hair was cut short like a military contractor's and his polo shirt and khakis looked like a relatively new purchase from JC Penny. His beard was greyer than his hair, and trimmed like a high school principal's, neat but not fashionable. The overall effect gave the impression that he was orderly but not obsessed with himself or how he was viewed by those around him.

"Danny," he said, smiling and extending his hand.

"Josh," Danny replied. "This is Laura."

"Joshua," he said, bowing his head slightly. "It's a pleasure to meet you."

He left my extended hand hanging there and sat down. Maybe it wasn't a bold enough gesture, especially given that he was almost a foot taller than me and my hand was well beneath his sightline. But I couldn't help thinking that if he was old school enough to believe that the earth was made in seven days some ten thousand years ago, he might be old school enough to think that men and women don't shake hands. Or maybe I was reading too much into it.

"Thank you for inviting me along," Joshua said in my direction, but not to me directly.

I stayed quiet.

"It was our pleasure," Danny said. "It's a nice coincidence, you being on the island at the same time we are."

"Yeah," I said. "What are the odds?"

"You'll have to forgive Laura. She's skeptical about everything. That's why we love her."

I shot Danny a look. He seemed to expect it, as his eyes moved from Joshua's face over to the bartender, avoiding mine entirely. In that moment of silence, the waves crashing against the shore could be heard, as well as the ding of the elevator. Saad and Duncan emerged and headed toward the bar, the former leading and the latter following with uncharacteristic reluctance. I've never known Duncan to hesitate when the doors to a pub were open to him.

T W O

In 1944, former American fighter pilot
Duane Hodgkinson was station [sic] in
Papua New Guinea during World War
II. As he and another military man were
moving through thick vegetation, they
heard a loud, startling sound. They came
to a clearing and a creature made a few
steps through the trail and took off. Duane
was astonished at the time because according to him, it was a "pterodactyl." It
[h]ad a long snout on it, a long appendage
coming out the back of its head, and great,
big wings.

— "Ropen," *Monster Wiki*

ON GOOGLE MAPS, UMBOI DOESN'T LOOK LIKE
much. The lush, small island lies across the Vitiaz Strait

from Papua New Guinea proper, pinched between it and the much larger island of New Britain. At nine hundred square kilometres, Umboi Island isn't that tiny in comparison to some of its neighbours. As we approached the eastern coast by boat, it appeared both pristine and majestic.

That morning we'd taken a small plane from Jackson's International Airport, at the northeast corner of Port Moresby, to Madang Airport in the port city of Madang. From there we chartered a boat to bring us to the island.

There were no tourist facilities or infrastructure on Umboi Island to support anyone more than the roughly six thousand people who lived there as farmers and subsistence fisherman. Outside of cryptozoological circles, the island was most famous for its volcano. A wave of fear and dread washed over me when I read about Umboi volcano. I had grown up close enough to Mount St. Helens that the threat of an active volcano was a clear and present danger, and my volcano phobia had followed me into adulthood.

The boat dropped anchor off the northwest coast of the island. We could see three figures standing on the beach. A Zodiac bobbed up and down in the waves halfway between us.

Umboi Island attracted tourists for snorkeling, swimming, diving, fishing, and daylight visits to coastal villages. It was devoid of beachside bars or resorts, and for that reason remained a valuable place to study the native flora and fauna — or in our case a bioluminescent flying creature, potentially a long-extinct pterosaur.

Known to Westerners as Rook Island in the first half of the twentieth century, Umboi Island had avoided the rapid urbanization that had sprung up around Port Moresby. Though sandwiched between the PNG mainland and the island of New Britain, Umboi was less visibly disturbed by Western encroachment. The interior was relatively untouched, with only a handful of larger villages on the island, all of which were located near the coast.

Residents relied on cargo ships to ferry them back and forth between Umboi and the mainland, and those ships were few and far between. Those that did service the island tended to sail around the southern part, making only one or two stops and leaving their passengers to walk for hours to their respective villages. There was Opai Beach at the southwestern end of the island and Lab Lab on the west coast. Higgins Point and Yangla were too small to receive ship traffic. Most of the other villages were not large enough to appear on any but the most detailed maps.

Fortunately for us, we were able to charter a ship to drop us off south of Opai Beach, past Higgins Point. With the bulk of the island covered with rainforest, and our trek to the U.K. team's camp an uphill one, it seemed wise to debark as close to our destination as possible — a luxury afforded to us by virtue of the fact that we worked for a massive media conglomerate.

We'd heard reports that a large storm hit the island in the days prior to our arrival, with violent winds and choppy waters making it near impossible to get a boat anywhere close to it. Fortunately, the severe weather had passed just before we arrived. I didn't really believe in luck, but I tried to recognize when things went my way and to be grateful.

During the trip over on the boat, Saad had seemed uncomfortable being on deck. The water in the Vitiaz Strait was relatively calm and there was no threat of being thrown overboard, no sprays of ocean water rising up over the hull. I think Saad had had his fill of boats and water in Newfoundland and was now content to busy himself watching the great frigatebirds soaring above us or staring at the approaching peak of the Umboi volcano.

Zach, our guide and liaison while we were on the island, was a wild-haired Australian we'd only met via online chats. He knelt in the prow of the Zodiac speeding toward us, chest out, like Washington crossing the Delaware, his long brown curls flying around in the wind as if they had a life of their own.

"Hey there!" Zach called out as he came alongside us. He tilted his head to the side and smiled. He had a conventionally handsome face, square-jawed and suntanned, but his eyes were concealed beneath blue-tinted Oakley sunglasses. And without the eyes, the picture is never complete. Clipped to the collar of his sky-blue T-shirt was a matching blue two-way radio with a black screen and antenna. The man operating the outboard motor, likely a resident of the island, didn't look up higher than the hull, focusing on his duties and avoiding eye contact with me.

As Zach turned to me, the sunlight revealed a scar on the side of his neck that contrasted with his deep tan. It was the size and shape of a quarter.

"Hi," I said. "I'm Laura."

"How d'ya do?" he said perfunctorily. "I'm Zach, this here is Gideon."

Gideon tossed a thumbs-up over his shoulder.

"This all your gear?" he asked, scanning the deck.

We were travelling light, but it would still require two trips in the Zodiac. As per our arrangement with our U.K. affiliate, there would be tents waiting for us at base camp, so it was really just a matter of ferrying my team and their bags, the camera gear, and a few crates of equipment to the beach. Smooth sailing across the water, but we still had to carry that gear up the steep rudimentary trail to the camp.

"You ladies want to come first, with the crates, then we'll make another round for the gents?"

We slid our equipment to the edge of the boat and handed each box down to Zach and Gideon. Once the crates were placed, Zach reached up and offered Lindsay his hand. She took it, climbing down into the Zodiac and taking a seat near Chris's camera equipment. All the trunks and crates and totes looked the same, but Chris's camera gear stood out because he had covered the case in stickers and decals, including one of the eye-atop-a-pyramid symbol from the U.S. dollar bill.

"You look after the all-seeing eye for me," Chris said, pointing at the crate and smiling at Lindsay.

"I thought I'd take it out and shoot some footage on the beach while we wait for the rest of you," she said.

"Don't you dare touch her," he said, a cartoonish angry look on his face, finger wagging.

Lindsay smiled for what might have been the first time on our journey. Her jet-black hair was tied neatly into a braid that hung between her shoulder blades, but a few loose tendrils had escaped during the boat trip and now whipped around her eyes. I should have realized that it was not going to be an easy trip for her.

I climbed down into the inflatable craft and took the seat across from Lindsay. The motor revved and we peeled away from the rest of the team and headed for shore. I quickly tried to map out in my head what I should say. Lindsay and I hadn't spoken much on this journey, or even since the end of the last one, so it was like starting over with her. But there was more baggage between us than in the Zodiac, and no sure way to unpack it. My dad used to say that the first step in fixing anything is figuring out if you should even try fixing it at all. He was a very handy man, but was keenly aware of his limits and knew when it was time to call in a specialist. I felt the need to talk to Lindsay, to help her through her troubles, but was afraid I would just make things worse.

As we approached the island, I watched as Lindsay raised her head and surveyed the majesty of it. I turned to take in the fast-approaching land mass, as well. It was magnificent, but it was also hard for me not to see it through post-colonial, Hollywood-influenced eyes. While I had hoped to dispel the myths that young-earth creationists often repeat, which seem rooted in notions that the South Pacific and Africa are remote regions out of Sir Arthur Conan Doyle's *The Lost World*, I, too, found myself thinking that any manner of fantastic creature could exist in such a place. But my inner skeptic quickly kicked in and took stock of how close we were to several highly populated areas. An island isn't "remote" just because it's far from what I'm used to. It struck me then how far I was from the familiar.

"First time in this neck of the woods, eh?" Zach asked over the sounds of the motor and the wind.

"Travelling for me was camping trips with my dad," I shouted. "Once I was old enough, and there was money enough to travel, well, there just wasn't enough time."

"You're here now, though, aren't you?" Zach yelled back. "I think you'll love it. It's an absolute paradise."

"That's high praise," I said.

"It's no Bondi, though," he said, smiling.

I laughed. I knew of Bondi Beach from television, and assumed it was the Australian equivalent of the Jersey Shore.

As we approached the beach, the clear water allowed us to see the bottom rising up to meet us. Zach hopped out into the knee-high water and pulled the craft ashore until it was firmly lodged in the sand. The man on the beach who had stood motionless during our crossing sprang into action, running into the water, giving the

Zodiac an additional push ashore before helping Zach and Gideon carry our equipment to the beach.

"This here's Jacob," Zach said, casting a nod toward the man. "He'll look after you until I get back."

Not needing to be looked after, I rose quickly, hopping over the side onto the wet sand. Lindsay handed me Chris's camera gear before climbing out of the Zodiac. Together, we walked over to where the other crates were being stacked. Jacob reached out to shake our hands and I noticed the same type of two-way radio as Zach carried clipped to his shirt.

Looking back out over the water to the boat, I took stock of the rest of the team — Chris, Duncan, Saad, Danny, and Joshua — awaiting the Zodiac's return. With the jungle at my back, the incentive to look out on the water was short-lived. The plant life, so lush and impossibly green, was so dense it appeared to be one solid mass. Only once I stared at it could I parse the moss-covered tree trunks from the vines and the thick, leathery leaves of plants reaching up from the forest floor. I felt a strange attraction to the jungle, a magnetic pull toward its rich biome. The long flights, the seemingly endless airport lines, the malaria medicine and vaccinations against yellow fever and typhoid, it had all been to get us here.

"I've waited for years to find myself in an ecosystem like this one," Lindsay said, surveying the treeline. "But ..." She let the word drift slowly to the ground like an autumn leaf.

"This isn't how you'd planned it," I said flatly.

"Searching for flying bioluminescent reptiles was never something I discussed with my guidance counsellor when charting my career path," she said with a laugh.

"Don't think of this as a detour," I said. "You're still on that path, this is just gaining experience and networking. It'll be good for the both of us to get to know the team from the U.K."

"I hope you're right," Lindsay said. "But I won't be able to show off my expertise in primates here, though, and I'm certainly not keen on sharing how much I've learned about cryptid folklore."

"Well, hopefully it'll be better than the last time you had to show off your anthropological skills by identifying human remains."

Lindsay shot me a dark look before turning her attention back to the trees. I'd crossed a line. While I mentally kicked myself, the roar of the Zodiac's outboard engine grew louder and louder. I turned to see the rest of the team rapidly approaching. Lindsay's solemnity and what lay behind it would have to be relegated to the back burner of my mind for the moment. We had work to do.

Zach hopped out of the Zodiac and pulled it toward the shore. The team then followed, jumping over the side one by one, Chris first, then Saad, Joshua, and Duncan, with Danny a distant fifth, his eyes scanning the water for crabs, jellyfish, or whatever other potential threat he saw in his mind's eye. He didn't waste any time getting to shore, last out of the boat but second only to Chris when it came to making it to dry land.

Aside from our chartered boat, Umboi Island only had two scheduled ships visit per week. They were both cargo ships, bringing the necessities that the islanders couldn't provide for themselves. As our ship left and made its way back to the main island, there was a sense that I was more cut off than I had ever been before. Tourist boats did occasionally sail through these waters, but for all intents and purposes, we were on our own.

Gideon, the leaner of the two guides, put his fingers to his lips and whistled, then waved down the beach. Three other men were soon hurrying along the pale sand. When they reached us, they exchanged words with Gideon in Papuan Kobai. One then followed Gideon back toward the Zodiac while the others looked to Zach, who indicated what they should carry. It wasn't a vacation for us, so I strapped on my pack and took a bag of gear in my hand and the rest of the team followed suit. Gideon stood ankle-deep in water as his companion climbed into the Zodiac, and soon the outboard again overpowered the sound of the wind and the birds riding its thermals above the shore. Gideon waved as the other man piloted the craft up the coast, and it was almost out of sight by the time we followed Zach onto a trail cut into the dense bush.

The breeze from the ocean was still on the back of our necks as the trail we followed rose gradually to a steep incline. Our base camp was located on a plateau toward the rim of the caldera, and I knew it would be a tough hike. The challenge made things easier, in a way, as I was less inclined to take in the scenery and focused entirely on the trek. Blue and red-and-black damselflies took off from green, leathery plants as we approached and fluttered in the air around us, only to land on plants ahead of us then move again. Heat seemed to radiate from each tree and fern the farther we got from the water.

Without the ocean breeze, the humidity took total control. The air was thick with moisture. It reminded me of moving through tropical pavilions at the zoo, except there was no condensation-misted glass door that led you back outside, away from the humidity. The whole island felt like a greenhouse, or a terrarium, and I wondered how long it would take me to acclimatize.

"You'll find reptile and frog species in this lowland rainforest you won't find anywhere else in PNG," Zach said, breathing heavily but maintaining a strong upward pace.

"Can the same not be said of most of the islands in the region?" I asked.

"That's true," Zach said, "but it takes all the fun out of it."

What started as a tight line of people, something that might have looked like a giant caterpillar from the forest canopy, began to stagger and spread apart. I kept pace with Zach as best I could, being no stranger to difficult hikes, but the rest of my team began falling back. The local guides were intermixed with us, with at least one at the rear of our train, so I wasn't worried that we'd lose anyone.

We approached a narrow clearing where sunlight reached down through the leaves and branches and butterflies danced between the beams of light.

"What d'you reckon, time for a breather?" Zach asked.

I felt the sweat rolling down my temples and pooling in the small of my back.

"Definitely time for a water break," I said.

The sound of laboured breathing caught up to us. Chris, who was in good shape, with a surfer's tan and grey flecks in his black hair, was closest to me. Saad followed quickly behind him, a look of determination — or competitiveness — on his face, not against Chris but against himself. Saad no longer seemed content with just being one of the smartest people in the room.

The rest of the team soon joined us and we stood in a circle for a moment, no one wanting to be the first to sit down. We were all frazzled and fatigued, tendrils of loose hair sticking to moist brows, sweat stains fanning out from our armpits. There's nothing glamorous about a scientific expedition, despite what old news reels and Hollywood movies might portray.

I set my bag and pack down and twisted the steel top off of my canteen. The team followed suit, except the guides, who stood together away from us. I turned to Zach.

"What's the protocol here?" I asked quietly. "Do the guides not take breaks?"

It was the first time I'd been in such a position. I was technically in charge of my team, but the guides worked for Zach. I didn't want to create friction for him, but I did want to make sure that everyone got a break and a chance to drink some water.

"They'll rest up when they're tired. This is nothing for them." He smiled at me before taking a long pull from his bottle. He was handsome in that outdoorsman way, with wild hair and a five o'clock shadow. There were two points on his skin, to the right of his jugular, just beneath his collarbone, the top of a tattoo just visible where his shirt opened. I've always been curious about what a person wants painted permanently on their bodies. Then there was that scar, an interesting story in itself, I was sure.

"You lot hoping to find the Ropen, eh?" Zach asked after pulling the bottle away from his lips.

"That would be something, wouldn't it?" I said.

"I'll say," Zach replied. "Can't say I've seen it m'self, although there's a lot out here at night."

"How do you mean?" Joshua asked.

Zach took off his hat, fanning himself. "Just that the sky seems to come alive at night. Stars, satellites, airplanes, comets, birds, bats, moths as big as your hand, it's all here. Then there're all the mozzies flying about. You've got to watch yourself at dawn and dusk."

"I should think bioluminescent pterosaurs would stand out, even amongst all that," Duncan said.

"You see strange lights out here every now and again," Zach went on, "too low to be airplanes, or so it seems. It's hard to be certain what you're seeing."

Two of the guides, Gideon and Jacob, were on their feet, in conference back along the trail. Gideon had a smartphone in his hand and was whispering to his friend while pointing at the screen. Neither spoke in English so I had no reason to pay them any mind. They were also on break as far as I was concerned, and if they wanted to watch a video on a phone that was their business.

"What have you got there, Gideon?" Zach asked.

I looked over at him, hoping my glance might dissuade him from interrupting the two men. He met my glance with his own, but all I could see was my reflection in his sunglasses. He waved Gideon over. The lean man, somewhere in his thirties or forties, walked through our group, his denim cutoffs exposing well-defined calves that flexed and rippled with each step over the uneven terrain.

Gideon said something in the regional dialect to Zach. I only recognized the word *phone*.

Zach turned to me. "You might be interested in this."

"My sons took this video," Gideon said. "I am no certain that it is what you're after, but I've not seen the like of it."

"This far out, a phone is nothing more than a camera and a flashlight," Zach said. "If you can even charge them. There are no cell towers here, no electricity even, unless you have a gas-powered generator or some modular solar charger."

I leaned in and Gideon tapped the screen to start the video. The footage started like a painting of various shades of charcoal before becoming so shaky that no shape could be defined. A strong wind provided the soundtrack, and as though mixed by Christopher Nolan, it stepped on the dialogue between Gideon's sons. The picture became more clear and amorphous blobs came into focus. Moonlight gave the scene depth and dimension. Trees swayed in the wind as the camera panned along a cliff edge, the darkness of the ocean in the distance. The camera operator then turned the phone inland to follow something over the treetops. Whatever it was emitted an otherworldly glow that seemed to fluctuate between pink and violet. It danced above the trees, pulsing in the air like a bioluminescent jellyfish or squid moving through water.

It was nothing like how scientists would expect a pterosaur to fly, but I had no idea what it was. Planes were the most likely explanation for the Ropen, but whatever was in this video certainly wasn't a plane. As it sank into the forest canopy, leaves and branches absorbed its odd light, taking on a strange, violet hue. Then the object, or creature, just disappeared.

Gideon was studying my face when I looked up, to gauge my reaction. Zach leaned toward me and took off his sunglasses, resting them on his hat. "So?" he asked. "What d'ya reckon?"

"I …" I shrugged my shoulders.

"Might I have a look?" Duncan asked, rising from a kneeling position and adjusting his glasses.

Joshua followed him over, and Gideon passed the phone to them.

Duncan replayed the video. Joshua leaned in, bracing himself with a hand on Duncan's shoulder, though the Englishman didn't seem to mind. The pair of paleontologists watched with the guarded fascination of scientists as the rest of us stood quietly. Saad, from a crouched position, watched them and then looked at me for some sign as to what the video contained, but I had no answers for him. Lindsay's mind was elsewhere, her eyes scanning the treetops then dropping down into the thick undergrowth. I suppose to her we were foolish, resting in the middle of a wondrous habitat, unique in the way many island habitats are, yet preoccupied with a low-resolution cellphone video, ignoring our surroundings. A bird call like a siren reverberated through the forest, causing us all to look up.

"A bird of paradise," Zach said. "Beats me which one, though. There are dozens of species here."

Duncan handed the phone back to Gideon, thanking him and bowing his head slightly. "That was interesting," he said.

"I'd like a copy," Joshua added. "I'd pay for it, of course."

"Gideon is more than happy to share it," Zach said.

"We would really appreciate a copy," I said to Gideon, so he didn't think we were all talking as though he wasn't standing before us.

"This is exactly what I'd hoped for," Joshua said, a smile spreading across his face. "This is one of the last places on earth where this creature could be spotted or even caught on video and not become an internet sensation. Who knows what else we might come across that no one outside of the island has ever heard of."

"Let's go," said Zach brightly as he lifted his pack and continued up the trail. Lindsay took my place second in line, and Saad followed after her. They struck up a conversation about the fauna on a tropical island. I walked with Duncan, wanting to hear his thoughts on the video. Joshua had the same idea, although he wasn't the type to let someone get a thought out completely before inserting one of his own.

"It was certainly an interesting bit of footage," Duncan said. "I'm reluctant to speculate as to what that was, but there was nothing to indicate that —"

"Interesting is an understatement," Joshua said excitedly. "Not to run off half-cocked, but that might be the best footage of a Ropen taken to date."

"That goes beyond jumping to conclusions," I said, rolling my eyes. "More like pole-vaulting to them."

Duncan smiled.

Joshua continued, unfazed by my doubt. "I admit it's far out, but that wasn't a bird, it wasn't a plane ..."

"And Superman's out of the question, I suppose," Duncan said.

I grinned. "We don't know what it was," I said. "But that's why we're all here."

An oft-repeated concept we hear in the world of cryptozoology is that of the "living fossil," the idea that some relict population of prehistoric creatures is out there somewhere, nesting in a cave shielded by the dense foliage of rainforests, untouched for millennia. The younger one presumes the earth to be, I suppose, the more likely it is that creatures found only in the fossil record might be out there in wild areas that have not been explored and catalogued by Western science. The very idea of a "living fossil," much like the "missing link," does not function within our current understanding of science. For Duncan and I, skepticism was warranted. For Joshua, who was still not convinced of Darwin's theory of biological evolution, the idea that a species might go on unchanged for eons was an easier pill to swallow. I knew not to press Joshua too much, or he'd likely counter with the example of the coelacanth, the cryptozoologist's go-to analogy when arguing that ancient creatures might still roam the earth, or swim in the deep oceans.

"And at least one of us is keeping an open mind," Joshua said mockingly.

I let that one slide. There wasn't any sense in explaining that believing in whatever suited one's biases and preconceptions was not being open-minded. Instead, I decided to shift gears. "Let's talk about what we saw in the video, maybe minds might change. What did you gentlemen think about how the thing flew?"

"After insects, pterosaurs were the first animals to develop powered flight," Duncan said. "Over the hundred and fifty million years they soared above the heads of dinosaurs, pterosaurs evolved into a wide range of sizes and shapes and adapted different behaviours. All that is to say there's no one way a pterosaur flew.

Whatever was in the video wasn't a plane, and it didn't flap its wings like a bat." He scratched his jaw where a few days' worth of stubble had erupted.

"I was going to point out the flight style," I said. "It swooped up and down, but no visible wing beats propelled it. It seemed to hover."

"Unfortunately, we have no sense of scale for the creature," Joshua said. "But its flight style seemed consistent with that of larger pterosaurs, such as Quetzalcoatlus."

Both scientists had made the study of Azhdarchidae, the family of the largest pterosaurs, an area of their research. Perhaps they were about to become best friends — or more likely, bitter enemies. I could tell by Duncan's body language that he was more invested in the discussion than he was in continuing forward toward our destination.

"You're referring to the marked absence of wing beats, I assume?" Duncan asked.

"I am. Larger pterosaurs, as you know, were more apt to glide along ocean currents of thermal uplifts, rather than waste precious energy flapping those massive wings."

"Many seabirds have that same flight style. It's far more likely, based on flight alone, that what we were seeing was a frigatebird."

"Frigatebirds don't emit a bioluminescent glow," Joshua said.

"There's no indication that pterosaurs did, either," Duncan replied.

"We wouldn't expect that there would be," Joshua said. "Fossilization is a rare enough occurrence, let alone the preservation of soft tissues, like the kind that would make bioluminescence possible."

Duncan rolled his eyes, but Joshua didn't notice as he kept his gaze trained on the path in front of him.

"Quetzalcoatlus was massive, fifteen feet tall or something like that?" I asked.

"Sixteen feet," Joshua said. "Its wingspan was between thirty-three and thirty-six feet."

"It's hard to imagine a creature like that soaring through the sky," I said. "How did it even get airborne?"

"Pterosaurs had hollow bones, like present-day birds," Duncan said. "They also had powerful limbs to launch themselves skyward."

"Imagine such an animal surviving the K-T extinction and staying relatively unchanged until now," I said.

"Crocodiles, frogs, and turtles have remained relatively unchanged," Duncan reminded us. "Although extant species were not the same as those competing with the dinosaurs, or hiding from them."

"There's the coelacanth," Joshua said.

Duncan shot me a quick smile.

I stifled a laugh and shook my head. "Yes, there's always the coelacanth," I said, sighing.

"They were considered extinct by mainstream science for sixty-six million years, until one was caught off the coast of South Africa in 1938," Joshua said. "Even you would say they haven't changed much in the four hundred million years in which you think that type of lobe-finned fish body type developed."

"Recent studies have shown that there's more diversity within coelacanth morphology than previously thought," Duncan said. "What we're looking for out here might not be the exact same as the pterosaurs you and I study, Dr. Laidlaw, but I believe they're closely related."

"I can honestly tell you that I would be delighted should that prove to be the case," Duncan said.

"If we find a glow-in-the-dark pterosaur, we'll be so famous that all the 'I told you so's' in the world would be worth it," I said to Joshua.

THREE

Two expeditions to Umboi Island in 2004
resulted in formal interviews with villagers and an expedition deep into the interior on the mainland in 2006 resulted in
indirect video evidence and a sighting by
two native explorers. Although no direct
proof has been presented, the indirect evidence is substantial and intriguing.

— Jonathan D. Whitcomb, "Reports
of Living Pterosaurs in the
Southwest Pacific"

THE TRAIL MEANDERED AS IT CLIMBED STEEPLY
toward the plateau. I imagined it was a mountain
stream and that any moment water might flow around
its bends. Then the idea of lava flowing downward

instead of water entered my mind. Pinching my eyes shut for a split second, I continued the upward trek.

At last, the sound of voices from above alerted us we'd nearly reached our destination.

Our U.K. affiliate's team had made camp on a plateau that faced west, a pair of buttress trees seemingly guarding the entrance, their massive root systems making them look like Lovecraft's Cthulhu. Ferns sprouted up between the roots from the rust-coloured soil. The camp itself bustled with activity as researchers moved from the tents where they slept to the tents where they ate, or the tents where they catalogued species of moths, butterflies, and beetles previously unknown to Western science. From the air, through the eyes of a Ropen (or more likely a frigatebird), the camp must have looked like an inexplicable patch of white laid over a sea of green and dark volcanic rock, a mysterious blight or moss overtaking a small piece of land.

"This is it," Zach said. "Home sweet home, or as I call it, Greenpatch Hill."

"On the map it says Butler's Plateau," I said.

"He's talking about *The Adventures of Blinky Bill*," Saad said.

"Hey, hey, Blinky Bill," Zach sang out. "Our cheeky mate from Greenpatch Hill."

"If you don't know him, you soon will," Saad continued.

"Good old Blinky Bill!" Zach and Saad sang in unison.

I hadn't given it much thought before, but since Pakistan is relatively close to Australia, English-language TV stations would probably source programs from there, not just from the U.S., U.K., or Canada. It was interesting to see this side of Saad. I don't think we'd ever discussed the TV he grew up on, and I'd never heard him sing.

"Eh, look what I found out in the bush," Zach said loudly as he passed through the natural gate formed by the trees and into the camp.

As though we'd stumbled onto a film set, and the director had yelled "cut," the research team stopped their comings and goings and moved into a semicircle to greet us. It wasn't the entire team, but enough that it made me feel welcome. I'd worried that we'd be the freaks, the black-haired, black-lipstick-wearing drama club students crashing a house party hosted by the homecoming queen. It might sound bizarre, equating biologists, entomologists, and the like with "the cool kids," but they were making a real difference in the scientific world, adding to the body of human knowledge. We, on the other hand, had come to make a TV program about a potentially ancient glow-in-the-dark flying creature, with our greatest challenge being to make the show memorable so that the viewers could apply scientific skepticism to their day-to-day lives. Or at least that had been the goal when I started the show. It was getting harder to know if I was actually close to achieving it.

We formed up in a line behind Zach, with Saad and Lindsay sticking close to me, Danny holding back slightly along with Duncan, Joshua, and Chris. Usually, Danny, being the natural-born schmoozer that he was, liked to insert himself into the mix first thing. There must have been a reason he wanted to stand back and observe the U.K. team.

"This is Laura Reagan, everyone," Zach said. "International TV sensation!"

The semicircle of scientists tittered and chuckled.

"Take a bow, Laura," Zach said.

It was difficult to tell if Zach was making a joke or if he seriously expected me to bow. I took it as good-hearted ribbing, because I sure as shit wasn't going to take a bow. Yet I couldn't help but feel a certain giddiness. It was like I'd made the big time. My dad had slept out of the back of his station wagon, staring through binoculars at still lakes or lush forests, looking for Champ or Bigfoot, and here I was in Papua New Guinea surrounded by scientists cataloguing new species. Wherever Dad was, I hoped he was proud of me.

"I think you'll recognize some of these folks from the telly, too," Zach said.

With the volcano rising in the distance as the backdrop, we began the round of introductions. Zach was right, I recognized three of the U.K. team members from clips of theirs I'd see online in documentaries. First was Dr. Kent McTavish, a herpetologist who specialized in frogs. He was in his early sixties, I'd guess, with a thin comb-over and a bushy beard that alternated between reddish and grey patches. He was mostly forehead, with narrow eyes and a broad, pinkish nose. Although he seemed lost as Zach was speaking, he came over and shook my hand warmly. "Welcome, welcome," he said heartily, continuing the greeting all the way down the line.

"Next is our bodgy James Bond, Aldo Middleton — he was SAS or something," Zach said. Middleton stood like a soldier at attention, wearing a tight-fitting Under Armour T-shirt and cargo shorts. His ice-blue eyes stood out beneath a fringe of black hair, and his right arm was covered in tattoos. He hosted several TV programs in the U.K., reality shows about surviving in the wilderness or challenging U.K. celebrities to endure basic training–style challenges.

"It was the Royal Marines, you Aussie tw—"

Zach cleared his throat and tilted his head toward me.

Aldo's mouth tightened and his nostrils flared. He then looked at me, bowing his head and forcing a smile. "A pleasure to meet you, ma'am," he said, his voice so deep and throaty it seemed he was putting it on for effect.

I wanted to put an end to the "ma'am" stuff immediately. "Please, call me Laura."

"Affirmative," he said. "On the condition that you call me Aldo." He smiled again, genuinely this time, before working his way quickly down the line, rotating through a set list of formalities, careful not to use the same one back-to-back.

Next, the famous wildlife photographer Brodie Campbell extended his hand, taking mine with the deft touch with which you handle an injured bird.

"Good of you to come," Brodie said, with his thick Scottish accent. He forced his eyes shut, seemingly embarrassed. "Don't know why I said that. Hello, welcome."

"Thank you," I said.

Brodie lingered a moment, planting his hands on his lower back and looking down at the dirt and leaf litter. It seemed as if there was something he wanted to say. The other field researchers were cuing up behind him.

"I look forward to seeing you work," I said. "I've watched several of the documentaries you shot. *Secrets of the Snow Leopard* was a wonder. I have no idea how you were able to get some of those shots."

His pale cheeks reddened, contrasting with his grey-white hair. "Ah, thank you," he said. "Perhaps we can have a chat later."

Brodie moved on to Saad, Lindsay, Danny, Duncan, Joshua, and Chris. The latter, before offering his hand, bowed to Brodie slightly. Being a fellow cameraman, Chris had an immense respect for Brodie's work. He and I had talked about it on the journey here, so I knew he might easily become starstruck.

Dr. McTavish had circled back around. "This is Celine Yi, one of our entomologists," he said.

"It's a pleasure," she said, her accent being what other Brits called "posh." She extended her hand, which was connected to a notably muscular arm. She had black hair haphazardly piled up on top of her head, a loose tendril plastered to her skin. She wore khakis and a navy-blue tank top. Her features reminded me of an actress but I couldn't remember which one. There was a certain Clark Kent geekiness to her to offset her model's face and CrossFit body fat percentage. Still, she wasn't like most of the scientists I'd ever met.

She smiled and gave a little nod before moving on. "And you're Lindsay," she said as she stood in front of our resident primate expert.

Lindsay seemed surprised that the woman knew her name.

Celine looked her up and down, then moved on to Danny, who set his charm to max when he laid eyes on her. Danny does this thing, which I can't stand, where he turns his palm skyward when shaking the hand of any woman he finds attractive. It's as though he plans to lift it up and kiss it. He never does, thank god, but he bows his head like he's going to. Some poor girl must have thought it was very charming back in the nineties or something, and he's stuck with the move ever since.

Celine placed her hand in his, quickly but not obtrusively rotating her thumb upwards and turning his hand with it. Had she seen that trick before? Was she sending Danny a message? I doubt he had the strength to rotate it back even if he wanted to.

"Pleasure," she said, moving on to Duncan and making another quick introduction.

"I'm somewhat of an entomology fan," Duncan said, stopping her before she moved on to Joshua. "By no means do I think myself an expert, but I've always loved beetles and weevils. It's a hobby of mine. Do you think we might see *Eupholus magnificus*? Maybe something from the genus *Chlamydopsis*?"

"Anything is possible," Celine said coolly, moving on. "We'll certainly keep an eye out, Doctor."

She made her way through the remaining introductions perfunctorily, shaking hands like it was the end of a softball game before rejoining her colleagues. As she mingled with the others she looked to me like a scientist as portrayed in a summer blockbuster about genetically modified sharks or something.

We were told the area on which the campsite was situated, Butler's Plateau, was named for some Englishman who had visited in the nineteenth century. I couldn't find that name anywhere outside of the map and material the network provided, but our British counterparts took it as gospel, so we went with it. If the people who lived on the island had a name for that particular spot, they weren't sharing it.

"All right, let's get you folks settled in, then we'll get a billy on boil and get our bearings," Zach announced.

Our group followed him toward two rows of large white tents, the kind you might host an outdoor wedding reception in, minus the fancy faux windows.

"Here's the ladies," Zach said, pointing to the tent on the left. "And there's the gents." He turned to face us. "The cots with the sheets bundled up in the middle are yours, I'll be in the mess when you're ready for lunch."

Danny, our producer and the point man for the network, set his bags down right there on the earthen floor, unzipping one and removing a satellite phone. It was an Iridium and had cost about a grand, but it looked like the first cellphone I ever owned, a Nokia, although thicker, sturdier. The rest of the men walked single file into the tent while Danny touched base with the network, letting Dina back at NatureWorld HQ know we'd arrived safe and sound. When we first set foot on the beach, I didn't even bother to check to see if my phone had reception. I just assumed we'd be out of contact with the rest of the world while we were here. But between the radios and the satellite phone, I realized that we'd be just about as "in touch" there as we would anywhere else. The only difference was response time. If we needed help, we'd be on our own.

Lindsay and I went through the mosquito netting and into the ladies' tent. Four cots were spoken for, lined up widthwise. The two empty cots were up against the length of the tent. We'd be sleeping head-to-toe, though the gap between the cots was comfortable. It was just a matter of deciding who wanted to be the closest to the entrance.

"Any preference?" I asked.

She moved as if she were sleepwalking, taking the cot nearest to the opening.

"You okay, Linds?"

"Yeah, I'm fine. Sorry, it's just …" She slid her backpack off her slender shoulders and let it fall, just catching it by one strap before it hit the ground. "This just seems wrong to me. It's what I've always wanted, but it just feels … wrong somehow."

Lindsay's plan had been to complete her Ph.D. and study primates in jungles similar to the kind found here, although not here specifically, as humans were the only primates on the island. But things hadn't gone according to plan. The Title IX investigation that resulted made Lindsay a minor celebrity, though not the kind anybody wants to be. Her Ph.D. adviser had been fired for harassment only after both he and Lindsay had been dragged through the media circus. After I found out what happened, I'd offered her a job on the show. We were obviously not conducting the kind of research that she was passionate about, but I thought that something was better than nothing at that point. But it seemed that getting her so close may have only reminded her how far she really was from where she wanted to be.

"All this *Creature X* work, it's only temporary," I said. "You'll be back at school finishing your degree in no time."

"For the life of me, I still don't know what I said or did that made him —"

"You didn't do a goddamn thing! You are in no way responsible for the thoughts, feelings, or actions of another human being, especially a grown man. And your Ph.D. adviser, for god's sake. He had the upper hand in that relationship."

"I know all that. I mean, I know that in the logical part of my brain. But …"

Her words hung in the air as she sighed.

"You'll think this is stupid, but I've always thought being a primatologist was, like, my *destiny*." She paused and studied my expression. I consciously kept every muscle relaxed and kept any look from my face. Lindsay seemed to only detect neutrality and continued.

"There's a traditional practice in Chinese families called Zhuazhou, where parents lay their one-year-old children down on a bed or carpet and surround them with various objects. According to the tradition, whatever object the child moves toward will determine their future career."

"So, if the child picks a stethoscope, they're going to be a doctor?" I asked.

"That's the idea. My mom, who is fond of telling this story, told me that once I had turned one, she and my dad had set me down on the carpet in our living room and surrounded me with all sorts of things — I'm sure a stethoscope was among them. Anyway, I started crawling toward a calculator, the big kind accountants used. But I kept going, leaving the circle of objects curated by my parents. I stopped at my dad's chair, reached underneath, and pulled out a ratty old toy monkey that my mom wanted to throw out but I had refused to part with."

"That's quite a story," I said. "Almost prophetic."

"I don't even know if it's true. It's not like I can remember. But my mother used it to make a case for studying anthropology in my undergrad. My dad wanted me to study something 'practical.'"

I smiled. "If it's your destiny, then it's your destiny," I said. "There's nothing to worry about. We'll get you back on track in no time."

Lindsay removed a strand of hair from her face. "You're telling me that you of all people believe in destiny?"

"I'm the girl that became a skeptic and science blogger to avoid following in my cryptozoologist father's footsteps," I said. "Look at me now."

FOUR

... two men saw a ropen clinging to a tree trunk. Having cut open and hung a game animal, the men believed that the ropen had followed the smell. The two demonstrated how the creature held itself in an upright posture — like a boy climbing a coconut tree — as it turned and looked down at them. (This posture mocks that of Flying Fox fruit bats that hang upside down from branches.) The ropen was about four feet tall with "hair" on its back.

— Jonathan D. Whitcomb, "Reports of Living Pterosaurs in the Southwest Pacific"

"I'M STARVING," DANNY ANNOUNCED.

It was 2:00 p.m. Papua New Guinea time. The team

had gathered outside the tents after settling in, grabbing some shut-eye, and changing into fresh clothes. The itinerary was simple: eat and rest, before heading out into the jungle. We still had hours of daylight, but most of our work would be conducted at night. The Ropen was supposedly nocturnal, after all. While Chris was filming the canopy, the trails, the thick palm leaves swaying, the rest of us would be setting up camera traps and survey nets. We hypothesized that the Ropen probably behaved similar to bats, therefore we'd use the same techniques conventional wildlife photographers used. We'd also be out at night, with infrared cameras and night-vision scopes, searching for whatever flew through the night sky above this tropical paradise.

Danny ushered us toward the mess tent where Zach was waiting for us.

When we walked in, I saw Dr. McTavish sitting at one of the folding tables. He wasn't so much eating the plate of noodles in front of him as staring at it as though it might become a piece of filet mignon through sheer force of will. Part of me was reluctant to ask him about Ropen, but as he had spent some time in the area, I hoped he might be able to shed some light on the cellphone footage Gideon had shown us.

"Dr. McTavish," I said. "I'd like to get your opinion on something."

He seemed surprised, as though he was suddenly in trouble, but stood up and joined our group.

"Aldo, I could use your eyes on this, too, if you don't mind," I added, seeing the TV host come through the tent opening.

"Certainly," he said, with the bearing of a man used to being told to go somewhere and do a job without asking why.

I played the video our guide had transferred to my iPad of the glowing object hovering over the trees. Dr. McTavish adjusted his glasses, leaning forward and squinting at the screen. Aldo stroked his finely shaved French beard with his thumb and forefinger.

"Can't say I've seen anything like that around here," Dr. McTavish said. "I've nae seen any bird or insect like that."

"Looks like a bloody drone to me," Aldo said. "Not military, one of those commercial jobs."

"I can't imagine a civilian coming all the way out here to fly a drone around," I said.

"Neither can I," Aldo said. "And I've never seen any of the fishermen in the village with one."

"Someone could be using one for research," Dr. McTavish said.

"Are there any other expeditions on the island right now, that you know of? Or was there during the past few weeks?"

"Only one," he said. "Though I've nae seen them using drones."

"Studying sea monkeys or something," Aldo added in his low grumble.

"Crab-eating macaques," Dr. McTavish clarified.

"It's not much of an expedition, really, just a pair of Yanks at the southern point of the island."

"Only one of them's a Yank," Aldo chimed in. "The other's Aussie."

"I wasn't aware that macaques were endemic to this region," I said.

"They're an invasive species," McTavish explained. "Some NGO sent those two here to study the impact their presence is having on the native species. The International Wildlife and Sustainability Foundation, it's called. The macaques have wreaked havoc on other islands in the region, so I don't suspect it'll be any different here."

"Havoc?" I asked.

"They're bad for humans, disturbing agriculture, but they're worse for birds, as they threaten critical breeding areas. They're as likely to raid nests as they are rice or taro crops. They have the dubious distinction of being on the World Conservation Union's 100 Worst Invasive Alien Species list."

"Have you met the researchers?" I asked Aldo.

"The Yank comes through here a lot, looking for company," he said, glancing toward Celine, who sat by herself at the end of the bench. "That one seemed to pluck him right out of the bush. She brought him back here like a lost puppy one night. I've seen the Aussie when I make my way farther south, toward the village, but he doesn't come around here."

"I guess some people take these jobs to get away from people," I said.

"Or maybe he can't stand his mate and just appreciates having the little research station to himself once in a while," Aldo said, laughing.

"I'd like to speak with them. They might have a better idea what this is. If it's their drone, that'll clear up the mystery."

"I'd be careful if I were you," Aldo said. "Up here, it's really just the creepy-crawlies you have to worry about. The closer you get to the water, though, the more you need your guard up against the people."

"Not the villagers," McTavish said. "They're a friendly sort."

"Who does that leave?" I asked. "I thought the island was relatively unpopulated. Surely you're not warning me about skin diving tourists?"

Aldo snickered, nodding as if counting the milliseconds for me to stop talking.

"Umboi is smack dab in the middle of a major drug trafficking route," he said. "Heroin and cocaine from Hong Kong shipped down to Australia by boats disguised as fishing trawlers. As I understand it, eastern European gangs have begun moving in on the action around here, too, to get in on the Australian market. It's big business."

"And these drug traffickers hide out on the island?"

"Typically, no. But when Coast Guard and law enforcement from Australia and the PNG Navy hunt these boats down, they've been known to take shelter in the coves or even abandon their loads on the islands if they feel their vessels will be seized or searched."

"It's not as if we've ever had a run-in with these men," McTavish said, giving Aldo a sidelong look. "I don't want to worry you."

"That's no reason to be careless," Aldo warned, shrugging. "If you want to go to the coast, just don't go alone. I'd be happy to escort you."

He didn't look like he'd be all that happy. He made it sound like I was just another civilian that he was burdened with. My father was like that, too, the military mixed so deeply in his blood that he saw a distinction between himself and everyone else, even once he was out.

"I wouldn't want to take you away from your duties," I said.

"I think Aldo is just trying to stay busy now that the shooting of the man-of-action part of the show is finished. At least, until the helicopter arrives, isn't that right?" McTavish looked at Aldo, no malice in his face, just the gentle ribbing of a somewhat awkward old scientist.

"Helicopter?" I asked.

"We're taking a short jaunt to New Britain tomorrow to study the butterflies there. Not the whole team, just Aldo, Brodie, Celine, and me."

There was a full brief on the U.K. team's activities among the mountain of paperwork the network had given me, but I'd only skimmed through it. A helicopter was a little beyond the budget of our show. The U.K. team's program was only three episodes compared to our thirteen for the season, with relatively the same budget, so they could afford to splurge where we had to make the money last.

"It's a safe bet that Yank'll come by tonight. You can ask him then," McTavish said.

"So, you say he's a regular around here?"

The two men looked at each other and smiled.

"Let's just say the bloke is a regular Lance Romance," Aldo said, winking at me.

"Laura!" Danny called from outside the mess tent, where he now stood with Chris, Joshua, and Duncan.

"Looks like it's time to go find your monster," Aldo said.

The rest of the team had apparently all finished eating while I'd been chatting with the two men. I grabbed one of the granola bars set out for us, tucking it into the pocket of my shorts before joining them.

Outside, the wind blew gently into the camp, leaves and branches swaying. Saad and Lindsay were nowhere to be seen. I listened for Saad's voice and picked it up over my right shoulder. He stood by the opening of one of the U.K. team's tents. Walking closer, I could see he was talking to a man who looked ten years older than us, with his hair shaved down to the grain and round cheeks, the flesh of them pulled back as he smiled broadly.

"My father loves test cricket," Saad said. "I prefer ODIs."

He turned as I came closer and smiled.

"Sounds like some kind of infection," I said.

"One-Day Internationals," they said in unison.

"This is Dr. Agahze," Saad said. "He's the lead herpetologist here."

The doctor wore shorts and the jersey of the English national cricket team.

Saad explained that inside the tent was where the U.K. team catalogued the flora and fauna they were collecting.

"Apologies for not attending the meet-and-greet earlier," Dr. Agahze said. "We've made an astounding discovery."

"That's perfectly understandable," I said. "I hope we'll get a chance to talk more about your work, but I'm sorry, Saad and I have to get going."

"Until later then," Dr. Agahze said.

The two men shook hands and Saad and I joined the others.

Lindsay still hadn't made an appearance. Her current mental state was not some adolescent melancholy, but the impact of trauma, and I had to keep reminding myself that the ocean breeze and tropical jungles weren't about to magically undo all that. Sometimes the most important thing a supportive ally can do is stop trying to "fix" the situation and just be there, just listen.

"Does Lindsay's mood seem off to you?" Saad asked, as if reading my mind.

"She's been through a lot," I said quietly. "I hoped that this trip might lift her spirits in a way that Newfoundland didn't, but being here only seems to remind her that her life plan has been derailed."

"Lindsay is a lot like me," Saad said. "She needs a project to dive into."

"Burying yourself in work to avoid processing your emotions doesn't seem healthy," I said.

"I don't mean I ignore the problem," he said. "But I approach it from a position of strength and confidence. When I feel adrift or powerless, it always helps me to solve a different problem or accomplish a different task. Makes me feel like I'm a capable person, that I can handle anything."

"You think I should back off, let her take the lead whenever possible?"

Saad narrowed his left eye and the corner of his mouth tightened. "I'm not sure," he said. "I don't know Lindsay all that well, but if we can find something that truly interests her, we should let her run with it."

"I just found out there are macaques on the island," I said. "Maybe we shoot a quick segment on invasive species and have her talk about them. If the Ropen exists, it's part of this ecosystem and could potentially be affected."

"I hate monkeys," Saad said. "Ever since one stole my backpack when I was a kid during a family trip in the north of Pakistan."

"I promise to keep the macaques away from you," I said, grinning.

He smiled. "They can be vicious, you know. And they stink!"

"Yeah, but I bet I'll smell worse after a few hours of hiking around in this heat."

Saad and I joined the others. Chris stood with his hand protecting his eyes from the sun, gazing up at the peak of the dormant volcano. Danny flashed his "time is money" look at me and I raised a finger before heading over to our sleeping tent.

Lindsay was sitting on her cot, looking down at her hands as though a phone or tablet should be there. She looked up as I came in. We stared at each other for a few uncomfortable seconds.

"We're heading out," I finally said.

She rose without a word and picked up her backpack.

We set out into the jungle single file, following Zach. Chris was filming our journey through the dense brush and up along a volcanic ridge. To our left was more foliage, varying shades of green, with the red bracts of the Heliconia breaking the monotony. Given their shape and colour, they are known as "lobster claws," which becomes perfectly clear the moment you lay eyes on one. To the right was a sheer slope that fell down into a valley, mist rising above the forest canopy.

"How long have you been coming to Umboi Island, Zach?" I asked our guide.

"'Bout ten years now, give or take."

"What brought you out here?"

"Brought me? Nothing specific, really. Just wanted some time away. It was a non-stop party back home, you know — surfing, booze, girls. One day I woke up and realized I'd never grow up if I stayed there."

"So, you set out on an adventure."

"Not quite. I got a job on a fishing boat. That didn't take, but I liked being out on the water, so a mate and I started a tour boat company. We made out all right, but the market was already cornered in Australia. So, we decided to try our luck here. Worked out for a while, but then my mate got homesick. I figured it'd be too hard to run the business without him, but there was still a market for a tour guide in these parts, so here I am."

As we ventured farther up the volcano, I thought of Duane Hodgkinson, the Second World War veteran who had wandered through this same jungle back in 1944 and returned claiming he'd seen what he referred to as a "pterodactyl." He and an army buddy had decided to go for a hike, and while out exploring, had come across a particularly large species of ant in a clearing. We're not talking giant ants, like from *Them!*, just larger than the two Americans had ever seen. It was while watching these ants that the men disturbed some brush, which startled a wild pig. Like some kind of Rube Goldberg machine, the pig's rapid departure flushed another creature, which Hodgkinson described as having a wingspan of about thirty feet and a horn-like appendage growing out of the back of its head. He said the grass and brush swayed from the force of the creature's wingbeats as it rose up from the edge of the clearing and flew away.

Hodgkinson's sighting occurred in broad daylight, so there was no mention of bioluminescence, not that a story so incredible needed it. It's unclear how long after the encounter Hodgkinson shared his account of it with anyone. There's also no record of his buddy coming forward to corroborate his story. Still, any rustle in the foliage got my heart racing just a little bit faster as I thought about it.

As we walked, we discussed the feasibility of camera traps and where to set up a lookout that would give us a good vantage point to observe the lower part of the island.

"Macaques are your thing, right?" I said to Lindsay as we climbed toward the rim of the volcanic mountain.

I wasn't sure she'd heard me at first, but she finally let out a deep breath and replied, "No, gibbons are 'my thing.'"

"So, basically macaques without the tails and crazy hairdos," I joked.

"Only the lion-tailed macaques have crazy hairdos," she said, but she was smiling.

"You seem to know a lot about macaques for a gibbon-fancier," I said.

"Where is this macaque talk coming from?"

"Well," I said, "apparently, there's an invasive species of macaque here. I heard there's a two-person team currently studying the impact they're having on the island's ecosystem. Since it's not far from the village, I thought we could drop in. From what I hear, the American researcher is the homesick type."

"You're not going to start questioning them about living pterosaurs, are you?"

"Lindsay, are you afraid I might embarrass you in front of your primatologist friends?"

She giggled, so quickly and quietly I couldn't be sure it even happened.

"I won't tell them that we met at a Bigfoot festival, then," I said.

"Hey! I was proving a point!"

"Okay, yeah, sure."

She made a fist and shook it at me. "I'd hit you if I wasn't afraid of your Tae Kwon Do skills."

"Saad!" I called ahead.

He stopped and turned around, his forehead glistening with sweat.

"Remember the night we met Lindsay?"

"Sure do. Roanoke Valley Rotary Club. She was hanging out with all those other Squatchers."

"I am not a Squatcher!" she said, feigning anger.

It was the most I'd ever seen her smile, and I'd spent days on end with her in Newfoundland and then back at NatureWorld headquarters in Maryland.

"And I don't know Tae Kwon Do," I said. "But I know enough to fake it, and I'd say the same for you about Squatching."

"I hate you guys," she said.

"You guys sound like you're having too much fun," Danny yelled from behind us. "No smiling. This is serious business."

I stuck out my tongue at him and saluted.

• ● •

When the cameras started rolling, we had to put on our game faces. We became more conscious of our posture, our word choices, the small ticks we each had when standing around. Even with all the beauty, the flora and fauna we might never see again, I was still aware that Chris was behind me somewhere, not exactly filming my every move, but pretty close to it.

As we hung the nets and set a few camera traps, I was reminded of the scene in *Predator*, when Arnold Schwarzenegger and his squad of glistening muscle men set a series of traps to kill the invisible alien antagonist hunting them for sport through the Latin American jungle. Although our biceps were far less impressive as we pulled nets into place or strapped the cameras onto the trees, there was a thrill about it. Contrary to the belief of many cryptozoologists, we proponents of conventional science would be thrilled to find a previously unnamed species, the weirder and more prehistoric the better.

"You know what this reminds me of?" Saad asked.

"*Predator*," Duncan and I said simultaneously.

"You owe me a pint," Duncan said, punching me in the shoulder.

"I'll buy you as many pints as you want at any pub on the island," I said, grinning. "You just name it."

FIVE

After numerous expeditions into the wilds of Papua New Guinea, Paul Nation believed he finally made the discovery of a lifetime in 2006. The Texas-born crypto-zoologist, explorer, and *"living-pterosaurs investigator"* came to the South Pacific Island nation to coordinate a search for a nocturnal flying creature known as Ropen. And on this fateful expedition, he believed he finally caught them on videotape.

— Dean Traylor, "Ropen: A Living
Dinosaur or a Figment of Faith?,"
Exemplore, December 31, 2020

IT SOUNDED LIKE A PARTY WAS UNDERWAY WHEN we finally got back to camp. The commissary tent was full of people and the sound of chatter filled the air, drowning out the night noises from the surrounding jungle; LED lanterns hung from tent posts, music played faintly.

Dr. McTavish emerged from the commissary with arms wide open. "We decided to throw you a little do on your first night!"

He was red-faced and I thought perhaps a little drunk, although I didn't see any booze around.

"You didn't have to do that," I said.

"Sure we did, sure we did," he said, turning toward the commissary. "Celine, be a dear and bring out some cups."

Celine emerged holding the handles of two enamel mugs in each hand. She didn't seem to me like the type to play waitress, but she looked unfazed. Dr. McTavish took a flask out of his back pocket and unscrewed the cap. Celine handed a mug to Saad and I, then to McTavish.

"Join me in a wee nip?" Dr. McTavish asked. "It's Scotch."

"Why not," I said.

He poured about a shot's worth into the mug.

"Celine?"

"Just a little."

"And for you, Saad?"

"No thanks," he said. "I don't drink."

"Well, we have some pop around here somewhere, for special occasions," he said, laughing.

McTavish was quick to tuck the flask back into his pocket. "I don't want me secret getting out," he said with a wink and a smile. "Ol' Brodie might drink me out of house and home." He touched his enamel mug to mine and Celine's before raising it to his lips.

"From what I've heard, drink is not his vice," Celine said before taking a sip.

"Aye," McTavish said. "I know the stories."

I inhaled the aroma of the Scotch before taking a sip. I didn't really have a taste for it, but I didn't want to miss out on the bonding opportunity with my U.K. colleagues. It burned a little going down before sending a warming sensation to the back of my throat.

"Cards," McTavish said quietly, as though we had asked what vice we were talking about.

"Also horses, slot machines …" Celine added.

"It's not a problem out here," McTavish said. "He's a straight shooter in the bush."

"Excuse me," Celine said suddenly, stepping back and heading over toward a group of her colleagues nearby.

"She's not one for idle gossip," McTavish said, giving me a wink. "She'll brighten up when her friend arrives."

I was curious to meet the man who could "brighten up" Celine Yi. I pictured him with a fitness model's body and five o'clock shadow, equally cold, equally distant, with the same poise. But time ticked by and Prince Charming didn't make an appearance at the ball. Saad and Dr. Agahze talked cricket, science, and Fortnite. Duncan and Dr. McTavish were becoming thick as thieves, sitting together in the commissary, their volume increasing with each drink. Danny worked his way into the thick of the U.K. team, shaking hands and making small talk. We were on the other side of the planet, but in that moment things felt familiar.

Looking up at the sky, at constellations I had never seen before, it struck me just how far I was from my regular life, my past, my home. I'd never felt so free. It was like I had no past, no parents, no baggage.

"Laura, won't you join us?" Duncan called out. He slid across the bench to make space. I sat down without a word, hoping I could just follow their conversation and insert myself unobtrusively. Like a kid in the schoolyard playing Double Dutch, I stood by and waited for my opportunity.

"That's a good question," Duncan said, turning to look at me. "When are we going to Loch Ness?"

"Soon," I said. "We'll be shooting a few episodes in the U.K. this season."

"I grew up in Lochaber," Dr. McTavish said. "Near Loch Morar, where legend has it a creature —"

"Morag," I said.

"That's right," McTavish said.

Lindsay sat down at the end of the bench, an enamel mug in her right hand. I shifted over slightly, not that she needed the space, but to show that she was welcome.

"Do you think we'll be able to visit that macaque research station?" she asked.

"I don't see why not," I said. "But you have to promise me that you're not going to send anyone your resumé."

Lindsay looked down at her hands.

"Hey, I'm just kidding," I said.

"I'd be lying if I said the thought hadn't crossed my mind," she said. "It's hard to get hired by these NGOs without a recommendation. It would be good for me to network."

"Then do it," I said, giving her a smile. "If you need a letter of recommendation from me, just ask."

"It's not that I'm not grateful for this job ..."

"It's your loss," I said. "When we find Nessie or the Yeti, you're going to be so jealous, right, Saad?"

Saad, who stood a few feet behind us, joined in without missing a beat. "You will rue the day you left us," he said.

"We're getting ahead of ourselves," she said, taking a long sip of her orange juice.

"Oy," Aldo said. "Your Yank has arrived."

He raised his arm in the air, goose-necking it at the wrist and pointing to a thinly built man with a head one size too large for his body who had emerged from the darkness of the jungle. As he walked into the light, I got a better look at his sallow face and circular glasses. If Celine was into him, well, he was certainly punching above his weight class.

Celine stood up and walked around the table to greet him, a million-dollar smile on her face. She walked right into his embrace and stayed there for a few beats, before turning back toward the commissary, taking his hand in hers. They sat down beside each other at the end of one of the benches.

"This is not possible," Lindsay said, her voice dropping an octave. I looked at her and saw tears welling up in her eyes. "This is not *fucking* possible!"

I followed her gaze to where Celine and her companion sat. They had both turned toward the sound of Lindsay's voice. The man seemed as staggered as Lindsay as he registered our presence. Celine gave him a sour look as he rose from the bench and took a few steps toward our table.

I looked at Lindsay. We were still very much strangers, though we had survived a life-threatening situation together. She was hard to read and kept her cards close to the vest. I appreciated that about her. But in that moment, her look of surprise, fear, and disgust, and the way those emotions rippled through every fibre of her, she was an open book.

"That's him? That's the guy?" I whispered.

She nodded; her face suddenly blank.

I'm a skeptic. That's not only my job, but who I am as a human being. But even I can't help but think the universe is a bitch. The odds of this seemed so astronomical that I could hardly believe it. What must have been going through Lindsay's head? It was like some kind of bastardized *Casablanca* — "out of all the research camps in all the world, that piece of shit had to walk into ours."

The man stopped a few feet from our table. He was not at all what I had pictured. Rail-thin and awkward, his Adam's apple protruding, his bony shoulders hunched. He reminded me of a vulture, and in a way that's what he was.

Saad, reading the situation from a distance, came over and stood behind Lindsay, who seemed frozen in place. I stood up and took two steps toward the man.

"Back off, Adam," I said sternly.

I saw motion over his right shoulder. Celine had stood up and started walking toward us. I let my peripheral vision track her, keeping my eyes set on the man in front of me.

"Back off," I repeated, lowering my voice but not my intensity. I was aware that creating a scene would only bring more attention to Lindsay, which she probably could do without.

"Lindsay, I —" He reached a hand out toward her and took two steps closer.

"Come any closer, Adam, and I swear to god, I will make you regret it!" I threatened.

There was movement from over Adam's left shoulder — a blur of muscle beneath an Under Armour logo. "Oy! Yank!" Aldo covered the distance with the smooth agility of a mountain lion. "The lady said back off, and if I was you, I'd take that advice before I explain it to you in the Queen's English." He raised his left fist up just under Adam's eye level. I'd watched Aldo enough to know that he was right-handed, so getting Adam to look at his left was just deception. As much as I wanted to see that right cross come into play, another part of me hoped Adam would just disappear into the jungle from whence he came and not spoil our shoot any more than he already had.

"Never got the schoolyard bully out of your system, did you?" Celine snapped at Aldo, reaching between the men and putting her arm across Adam's chest. "I thought the army was supposed to drill that out of you!"

She pulled Adam away and led him out of the commissary and across the well-trodden ground of the camp. The pair kept walking until they disappeared into the shadows, Adam's white shirt the last thing to blink out as the jungle engulfed them.

I turned to Aldo. "Thank you."

He smiled without showing his teeth. I liked to do my own macho posturing, but you couldn't argue with the results. I'd rather have Celine angry with another member of her own team than have her angry with mine. "So, your mate already knows that Yank?" he asked.

"Unfortunately."

"Want to tell me about it?" He was standing very close to me now, hands on hips, his broad shoulders rolled forward. Aldo was by no means huge, but he was well muscled and thickly built, more football player than powerlifter. He seemed very aware of his presence and honed it for effect.

"No," I said. "I don't."

I turned to Lindsay and said quietly, "Let's go."

SIX

Throughout history, every major culture has stories of reptilian monsters who threatened their livelihood. From Egypt to India, and even the Sioux Nation, tales of these flying dinosaurs or winged lizards have filled the cultural imagination of societies throughout the ages … Today there are still accounts of reptilian monsters said to haunt and harass villagers throughout the remaining corners of largely unexplored forests …

— Shalee Britton, "Hidden in Plain Sight: The Pterodactyl of New Guinea," *Ancient Origins*, February 3, 2021

WE RETURNED TO THE RIDGE THAT NIGHT, OUR headlamps penetrating the darkness that surrounded us. The air was cooler now, but a damp warmth still radiated up from the ground beneath us. As we climbed higher up toward the ridge, I felt the salty breeze from the ocean and inhaled deeply.

The unpleasant memory of Adam's appearance at the camp still swirled around us. It was hard to take a glow-in-the-dark pterosaur seriously. It was like we'd been staked down to the earth, the weight of real life prohibiting the flight of fancy that is cryptozoology.

"Hey, Zach, where did those boys shoot that video?" I asked, breaking the uncomfortable silence. "Anywhere near here?"

"No. It's more to the east of the island," he said, chopping the air with his hand, his fingertips pointing across the valley at the base of the ridge, not directly toward the ocean but diagonally across the southern portion of the island. "But not too far, less than an hour. I could take you there now if you want. There's a trail up ahead that leads up the mountain and passes above the village right to the spot."

"That seems like the logical place to start our search, as we'll definitely be discussing the sighting on the show," I said. "The camera traps and the survey nets work better if we're not hovering in the same vicinity anyway."

"Is it safe to travel that far at night?" Saad asked.

"It's well-travelled, widely used by the locals, but I wouldn't recommend taking it alone, or if you're unfamiliar with the terrain," Zach said. "Lucky I'm here, eh?"

Our camera traps and nets now set, the team followed Zach to the trail. If the creature was real, and
I, of course, was highly skeptical of that, we'd have a
good chance of catching it on camera. The legends
and eyewitness reports varied so much, from Duane
Hodgkinson's diurnal pterodactyl to the creature prey-
ing on villagers and their dead at night, to the smaller
flying reptiles seen flying out to sea to fish along the
reefs. Dad taught me that every creature moves in a
circle, with its home and its food supply being the two
keys to hunting it. Legend has it that the Ropen roost
in caves high up near the crater of the volcano. We had
yet to come across any caves, and with the conflicting
accounts about what the creature eats, it was hard to
predict where it might go once it left the safety of its
nesting area. But it, or they, would likely have to de-
scend to lower altitudes to find prey, so hopefully we'd
catch a sighting on one of its nightly forays.

I wasn't holding out hope, since, as I mentioned, I
didn't really expect to find the creature. Or did I? Was
Joshua's conviction rubbing off on me? Or was it really
a case of *like father, like daughter*? How much of my
skepticism was just to convince myself that the creak-
ing floorboards and quick flashes of movement caught
out of the corner of my eye were perfectly explainable
and nothing to fear? I wanted to have my father's sense
of curiosity, his wonderment, but I couldn't find that
without opening up my mind to the possibilities.

The older I got the more I understood the silent
treatment Mom gave Dad when he came back from one

of his road trips — his "expeditions," as he called them. When I was a girl, it seemed like it was Dad's life work, his calling, his dream, that Mom was trying to quash because she craved the boring domesticity of the families she saw on TV. How could a kid understand that her mom was watching her husband drift farther and farther away from his family and reality? I couldn't help but wonder if Dad might have fallen in with QAnon had that conspiracy quasi-cult been around when he got out of the army and found himself adrift in civilian life. What would I even say to him if I were to see him again? I had stopped understanding the pull that was inside of me, the homing instinct to find my father. If he wanted to, he could reach out to me, couldn't he?

The jungle orchestra rose to a crescendo as night settled around us. The trail took us up and above the jungle as it wound up and around the mountain. We were able to look out over much of the southern part of the island, a wall of rock at our backs. The trail was narrow here, but thankfully a tangle of dense shrubs formed a natural barrier between us and the edge, which dropped off sharply into the blackness below us.

We noted that there were fissures in the rock wall, and the light from our headlamps revealed narrow caves that seemed to stretch deep into the mountain. A volcanic island was likely full of them, magma chambers that belched hot lava out onto the surface and down the steep slopes.

Lindsay slowed down to take a closer look at the fissures, peering into the darkness, looking as though she could see something the rest of us couldn't. Chris was further behind, filming the hillside with the night vision camera, and Danny walked slowly beside him. It was almost as if the team was organized by zeal, except for Zach, who led because it was his job.

"What's that?" Joshua asked suddenly.

He hadn't been examining the caves with us, but instead was searching the treeline at the bottom of the ridge with his infrared scope.

"What's what?"

"There's a ball of light on the scope."

Duncan, Saad, and I moved closer to Joshua and turned off our headlamps, trying to find out exactly where he was looking. He lowered the scope and pointed across the valley, toward a ridge on the other side. There was a faint glow, almost invisible in a valley awash in starlight. He passed me the scope and through it the orb of light became much clearer. But I noticed the glow was stationary, so definitely not a flying creature.

"It looks like a campfire," I said.

"Out here?" Joshua asked.

"We're not the only people on the island," I said.

"It should be simple enough to confirm in the daylight," Duncan said, "supposing anyone wants to hike out there in the morning."

Zach joined us and peered down over the edge of the steep ridge.

"We're picking up a heat signature," Joshua said excitedly, handing over his night-vision scope and pointing in the direction of the faint glow. "Any idea what it might be?"

"A campfire, I reckon," Zach ascertained after just a few seconds.

If Joshua was dejected, he certainly didn't show it, and seemed content to let it go and move on.

We continued along the path single file, Saad and I trailing behind. Soon the treetops sunk away as the ground sloped more steeply toward the ocean. Near the coast, the light from kerosene lamps and cooking fires became visible, revealing the location of the village below.

"Umboi Island seems like the polar opposite of Lake Crescent," Saad said. "Is that the reason you picked it?"

"Actually, yeah … I have to level with you, Saad. I hired a private investigator to find my dad."

He stopped instantly, and I nearly ran into him. "What?"

I pulled him back as he started off again. I didn't want to risk Danny and the others overhearing what I was about to say. In the dark, everyone kept an ear out.

"Robert's Arm was my dad's last known whereabouts, so that's why I wanted to go to Lake Crescent. Cressie was the last cryptid my dad went searching for when he left my mom and I. I hoped maybe he'd settled down there, or left some trace. But none of the people we met who Dad would have reached out to, the experts or eyewitnesses, had heard from him. Maybe he never made it that far. My PI hasn't found out anything more, and neither have I."

We took a few steps in silence.

"Why didn't you tell me?"

"I don't know. Part of me was … embarrassed, almost ashamed. I don't know. The guy walked out on my mom and me when I was a teenager, yet I follow in his footsteps at every opportunity. It's kinda pathetic."

Saad stopped again and looked back at me. "It's not pathetic to want to find your family."

"But maybe Dad doesn't want to be found."

"So, why did you choose to come here?" he asked.

"For the exact opposite reason. I wanted to go to the farthest place possible. Dad spent the better part of a decade in our station wagon, driving from cryptid sighting to cryptid sighting. From Bigfoot to the Michigan Dogman, to Champ and the Mothman, crisscrossing the U.S. and even going into Canada in search of Ogopogo, Igopogo, Old Ned, and Cressie. I wanted to go to a place where he'd never been, a name I'd never heard him and my mother fight over as she tried and failed to stop him from leaving again."

"I can tell you miss him a lot …" Saad said, letting the words evaporate between us.

"I wish I didn't. I'm not able to bury him in some basement inside myself like my mom has. I'd like to hate him. If he'd settled down and started a new family, maybe with a much younger woman, and had a whole litter of little kids who he doted on, then I could hate him comfortably. But sometimes I lie awake at night and fear the worst. I knew nothing about Gulf War Syndrome as a kid, or PTSD. But now I think about all the long drives he took, all that time he spent alone out on the highway, or in the woods, or on the water. Anything could have happened to him …"

Three beams held steady in front of us, pointing in vaguely separate directions but blending as they diffused into the blackness as Zach, Duncan, and Joshua waited for us to catch up. Danny, Chris, and Lindsay were somewhere in the darkness behind us.

"There's a river that cuts into the limestone and runs down the side of the mountain out to the sea," Zach said. "The object in the boys' video seemed to be following that river." He pointed to where the trail branched off, with a long, winding path leading down through the trees toward the village, the other up into darkness and the looming crater.

"We're heading down that way, but take it slow," he said. "There was a bridge over the river, but it was washed away during the storm. Technically, this area is strictly off limits."

"That sounds like the kind of thing you might have warned us about ahead of time," I said.

"No need," he said. "I'm here, aren't I?"

"But you can't show us where the video was shot and warn Lindsay, Chris, and Danny, can you?"

"We can wait here for the others, together, or you can continue on down the trail and we'll catch up. It's up to you."

"Come on, Saad," I said, starting down the trail.

We couldn't see any river, but we took Zach's word for it that it was there. As we descended, moths and other bugs criss-crossed through the beams of our headlamps. Soon, I began to hear the sound of rushing water and then the trail suddenly opened up and began to follow along beside the bubbling torrent.

After another twenty minutes the trail began to level out, the descent much more gradual than before. The trees had risen up around us once again, the canopy branching up, umbrellas of varying heights that cut us off from the starlight. Zach had yet to catch up. Saad and I turned around and scanned the trail for the beams of our teammates' headlamps, but there was nothing but blackness and the shimmer of the starlight off the water.

"Could we have gotten that far ahead?" Saad asked.

"That all depends on the hill, I guess. They might be taking it very slow, whereas we might not have been as careful and let gravity take us down faster."

I unclipped the radio from the strap of my backpack. Even though they were out of sight, it was impossible for Zach and the others to be out of radio range.

"You slowpokes coming, over," I said into the blue-and-black radio.

"Laura!" Saad hissed, smacking my backpack and pointing up. "Turn off your headlamp."

I did as he said and as my eyes adjusted to the blackness of the night, I caught a glimpse of several violet lights that whirled in a gap in the forest canopy. The lights were visible for only a split second before disappearing from view.

"The hell?" I yelled. I clipped the radio back to the strap, turned on my headlamp, and took off as quickly as I could manage down the winding trail toward the point where the lights had disappeared. It was as though I no longer controlled my own legs.

"*Skyline*," Saad yelled, then, "Laura, wait up!"

Saad was right, it was like *Skyline*, a cheesy sci-fi flick we'd watched together on his laptop while we were still in school about an invasion force of glowing blue-and-purple alien spacecraft that hypnotized humans to come toward them like moths to flame. The difference was, my mind wasn't being controlled, I just saw something that needed to be chased. Simple as that.

Some reports stated that the Ropen flew out from its mountain lair to fish off the reefs at night. Whatever I was chasing was heading for the open water from the mountain. Only the tiniest amounts of light bled between the leaves and the branches, but we were running out of trees, of land. Once that glowing object was out over the water, I'd be able to get a good look, assuming it wouldn't put so much distance between us that it would only be an orb in the sky.

Suddenly, my boot sunk into something squishy, my momentum pulling me forward and sending me flying. I landed hard and careened along the trail like it was the Crocodile Mile.

"Laura!" Saad called out from behind me.

I rolled over onto my back to warn him, but that wasn't necessary. I could see the beam from his headlamp slow as he approached. Saad was always the more patient, more cautious one.

"Are you okay?" he asked.

"Safe!" I called out, making an umpire's sweeping arm gesture.

"You scared me," he said, softly and frankly.

"I scared myself there."

Saad gave me a hand up out of the mud.

"Laura?" a voice squawked over the radio, which had separated itself from my backpack as I dove into home plate.

Saad located the radio and wiped it on his shirt before handing it over.

"I'm here," I said, still breathing hard.

Our colleagues soon appeared out of the pitch-black of the rainforest, their train of beams like oncoming headlights. I did a quick self-assessment, the mud on my clothes, potential bruises on my knees, scrapes on my elbows. Wounded pride was the biggest injury, but my game face was on before the others got close.

"What the hell happened to you?" Danny asked.

"That glowing object in the sky that the boys filmed? Well, we just saw it."

It was well past two in the morning when we decided to call it a night. The camera traps we'd set could do the rest of the work. I was dirty and tired and had no desire to stay on my feet a second longer. We'd planned an early start the next morning and had factored naps into the schedule. We would sleep for four hours, then start out for the village to speak with some of the locals who claimed to have seen the creatures their ancestors had dubbed "Ropen."

I was trying to stay close to Saad, my legs a little stiff around the knees from my fall, but I had a pterosaur expert on either side of me. Joshua, for confirmation bias reasons, was the one hounding me, but Duncan didn't want to miss out on anything that I might say. But I didn't feel like talking about it.

"What can you tell us about the creature's flight? Was it soaring just above the canopy, or higher in the sky? How fast do you think it was travelling?"

"I don't know that there was any creature, Joshua," I said. "All I saw was a light that moved toward the water."

He pulled away and sidled up to Saad, who was three paces ahead. "What did you see?"

"It's a shame that we didn't get the light on camera," Duncan said sulkily.

Mysterious lights on camera are always good TV. I pictured the low-lit video lab, the expert in glasses zooming in on the lights or slowing the frames down. We've seen it a thousand times in series like *Creature X*. Even if we could prove definitively that the lights were not a Ropen, it was entertaining to see the detective work play out.

A warm wind met us head-on as the forest rose up around the trail and we lost sight of the smooth darkness that was the distant ocean. The trail narrowed and we proceeded single file. Somehow, I became the leader even though I was sore and moving slowly.

"Don't move," a voice hissed from the forest ahead. "Not another step."

I froze in place, my arms out as a signal to the others coming up behind me.

"What's the hold up?" I heard Danny say from the back of the line.

A figure suddenly emerged from the wall of shadows, startling me. I soon recognized it was Brodie, holding his camera like it was a submachine gun. He wasn't pointing it toward us, but at the ground in front of us. He took one hand away from his camera and reached for his two-way radio. "Aldo, bring the snake hook up the north trail, and bring Brian."

"Everybody keep still," I said, shining my beam along the ground.

"Brian" was Dr. Agahze, the U.K. team's herpetologist. That told me all I needed to know, as if Brodie's mention of a "snake hook" wasn't a dead giveaway. I could feel the tension in the team as we stood there silently holding our collective breaths.

With how the hill sloped and the foliage between us, I couldn't see what Brodie was pointing his camera at. I thought I heard a slithering sound in the brush, but that might have been my imagination playing tricks on me. My own heartbeat started counting time in the side of my neck just below my ear.

After what seemed like an hour, Aldo arrived holding the snake hook as though it was his rifle and he was back in the Royal Marines. His fitness level was apparent when you looked at him in the daylight, but was now made clearer by the lag in how long it took Dr. Agahze to catch up to him. The herpetologist seemed winded from the uphill sprint, whereas Aldo looked eager for more as he looked through the leaf litter in the direction Brodie pointed his camera.

"There," Brodie hissed, "about two metres ahead of me."

"Small-eye?" Aldo asked.

"Might very well be."

"The small-eyed snake is quite venomous, I read," Duncan whispered from behind me.

I bent my knees a little and moved up onto the balls of my feet. I didn't want to get caught flat-footed if the snake made a move toward me.

"There are also some very similar species around here that are not venomous," Dr. Agahze added.

"I'll keep my fingers crossed that it's one of the non-venomous ones," I whispered, still unable to see the snake from where I stood.

"Would you look at the size of that!" Aldo exclaimed. "Laura, have your team back away … slowly, please."

Aldo came toward us in a half crouch, the snake hook out in front of him like a spear.

"You heard the man," I said, summoning a little bass in my voice. As a rule, I am not afraid of snakes. I do, however, have a healthy disdain for anything that can kill me once it's within striking distance. That is made more urgent when I can't see the damn thing.

We backed away slowly, as though we feared what Aldo might do, none of us able to see the real threat on the ground between the Englishman and ourselves. The snake hook looked like something The Riddler might use as a walking stick, although the hook at the top that was curved like a question mark was slightly too flat. I knew it was that flat end after the curve that was used to press the snake into the ground so that one might grab the back of its head and handle it safely.

Aldo held the snake hook low to the ground, his eyes searching the leaf litter. Suddenly, the snake slithered out onto the path in front of me. I froze, not breathing. Aldo moved deftly, but not so quickly that he might break the snake's neck. As my martial arts instructor says, "smooth is fast." Aldo's technique was so practised, his movement so fluid, that he had the hook placed perfectly on the base of the snake's skull as though a frame had been skipped. First it wasn't there, then it was, no intermediary. I let out my breath slowly.

With the hook safely in place, Aldo bent down, taking hold of the back of the snake's head, rendering it harmless so long as he had it within his grasp. The snake tried coiling in midair, then seemingly understanding the futility, hung there limply as though it were dead. Aldo used his free hand to scoop up the snake's body, bringing in toward Dr. Agahze like it was an offering of fine silk.

"You'll need more than a plaster if this one gets its fangs into you," Aldo said.

"Would you look at this beauty," Dr. Agahze said. He pulled a measuring tape from his pocket and held it parallel to the snake, tip to tail. He checked and rechecked his measurement, then let out a whistle. "Just shy of two metres," he said. "The name for this snake in Western Papuan is *ikaheca*, which translates as 'land eel' on account of its preferences for damp habitats, swamps, wetlands, or in this case, rainforests."

"We've had enough of eels, haven't we, Laura?" Danny said, his voice sounding a bit shaky.

Our trip to Lake Crescent was still fresh in my mind, as well. All the trouble over a mythical eel, then all the trouble caused by a real one. But I hadn't forgotten Danny's role in that mess.

"I don't know, Danny, I've seen slimier, more slippery creatures."

I watched as Danny turned to Chris and mouthed the word "ouch." Chris pulled his face away from his camera and chuckled.

"Exactly how venomous is that snake?" Duncan asked.

"They're highly venomous, lethal to humans. A slow death, too — fever, abdominal pain, nausea, vomiting, spontaneous bleeding. But it's the respiratory paralysis that kills."

"Lovely," Duncan said flatly.

Brodie took some nice shots of the snake up close, while Chris filmed the procedure from afar. It wasn't a Ropen, but the footage would satisfy our science-based audience, as well as those tuning in just to potentially see a monster. Our world is full of fantastic, sometimes frightening creatures. We don't need bioluminescent pterosaurs; we have enough amazing animals that fit within our understanding of Darwinian evolution and geologic time.

"Laura," Aldo said. "Get your team clear, then I'll release this little beauty."

"You have an odd definition for both 'little' and 'beauty,'" I said.

He took three steps off the trail, offering the snake to the jungle now. I waved the others through. Saad, Lindsay, Zach, Joshua, Duncan, Danny, and Chris moved past the snake handler at varying paces.

Brodie and Aldo joined in behind us, forming a rear guard as we returned to camp. Headlamps and starlight guided us back. Dr. Agahze sidled up beside Saad as they navigated the trail, fast friends.

"Thank you for the heads-up back there," I said to Brodie.

"'Twas nothing," he said.

"Still, we're lucky you happened to be out here."

He shrugged.

"Are you often out alone at night? It seems dangerous," I said.

"There're too many nocturnal creatures about to not shoot at night," he said. "As for going out alone, well, I don't need anyone nearby scaring animals away now, do I?"

"Good point."

"So, gonna tell me how ye got that streak of mud down yer front?"

The lights of the camp were now visible. The U.K. team was active twenty-four hours a day, on rotating shifts, to study both the diurnal and nocturnal creatures of the rainforest. Fortunately, nothing was expected of me for the next few hours.

"No, I don't think I will," I said.

Brodie looked to Saad, who shrugged and smiled at the famed wildlife photographer.

As we entered the camp, the team scattered in several directions, leaving only Saad and I standing between the tents. We decided to walk to the edge of the plateau, near the trailhead that led back down to the beach where we'd landed. Although I had been dog-tired earlier, I was now wide awake.

"We really should sleep," Saad said.

"You're right. But just because we should doesn't mean it'll just happen."

We stopped just short of entering the jungle. The subtle droning of insects seemed to fill up the emptiness of night. There was a crack in the distance, a branch snapping under the weight of an animal passing over it.

"I suppose the show wouldn't be any fun if we stayed local just to avoid jet lag," I said. "We could go from lake monster to lake monster, ape man to ape man, and never leave the States, but …"

"What did we see back there?" Saad asked.

"I wish I knew."

More than that, I wished my dad had been there to see it.

SEVEN

… by the time the tug tracked down the vessel it had drifted hundreds of kilometres north into the waters around the Siassi Islands, an area so unsettled that the only outside visitors are usually dinosaur hunters searching for a mysterious pterodactyl-like creature the locals call the Ropen or flying devil, which some have suggested is the last living dinosaur.

— Rory Callinan and David Murray,
"Paradise Lost to a Dirty Trade,"
Australian, September 10, 2018

ZACH MET US IN THE COMMISSARY THE NEXT morning, his unkempt but rested look giving the impression that he was perfectly comfortable here, in his element. Whereas my team slogged through the camp like zombies, stretching, limping, and working the kinks out after too-little sleep on the uncomfortable cots, Zach looked fresh and eager to get moving. Jacob and Gideon were waiting for us in the village, he told us, having gathered several eyewitnesses who claimed to have seen the Ropen — a few elders and Gideon's sons. The rest of the village would be hard at work, mostly fishing, some logging and foraging in the interior of the island.

"How are you feeling?" Lindsay asked, entering the commissary behind me.

"I slept just long enough to heal a little, but not long enough to really stiffen up," I said. "Thanks for asking."

"Sure," she said.

Zach came over and tipped his Tilley hat. "Let's get you some brekky before we hit the road," he said, somewhat redundantly, as we were all there to eat.

Joshua and Duncan were notably absent. Zach traced my gaze as it swept over the camp. I had a hunch where they might have gone, but it was possible they'd snuck into the tent where the U.K. team were cataloguing their finds. They were, after all, curious scientists.

"Your Indiana Jones went off first thing, the English paleontologist in tow," Zach said. "Don't worry, Aldo is minding them."

I looked over at Danny, who was already digging into his breakfast. "Did you know Joshua and Duncan were off on their own this morning?"

Feeling my gaze on his face, he deliberately stared ahead, chewing on his porridge, nodding all the while.

"Josh ran it by me before he left," he said once he'd swallowed.

"They're looking around that area where he spotted that heat signature, aren't they?"

"It's a short walk from there to the main trail that will take us to the village," he said. "We'll rendezvous with them on our way and won't miss a minute of shooting time." There would come a point in time where I'd have words with Danny about his undercutting my authority. I was a newbie as far as TV went, and he was there to mentor me on behalf of the network, but it was understood that I was calling the shots. He snuck hiring Joshua past me, which might be almost as bad as the stunt he pulled in Lake Crescent.

"Granola?" Lindsay asked, handing me one of the individually wrapped packages that motels serve as part of their continental breakfasts.

"Sure. Thank you."

We sat down together at the end of the bench as far from Danny as possible.

"I just wanted to say that I appreciate the way you stuck by me," Lindsay said.

"It's nothing."

She leaned in and lowered her voice. "No, it's definitely something. When I first complained about Adam, about his advances, nobody wanted to listen. People would scatter when they saw me coming. I felt that no one was on my side. What was worse, though, was that no one wanted to take any kind of a stand. It wasn't that they didn't want to support me personally, they just didn't want to do anything except look the other way." She paused, crunching her granola. "It means a lot that you took a stand last night," she said. "You didn't even hesitate."

"You're my co-worker and my friend," I said. "I told you before, I have zero tolerance for this kind of thing. Now that we all know what this guy looks like, we won't let him anywhere near you."

She gave me a little nod and punctuated it with blink. If that meant what I thought it did, I was happy. I wanted Lindsay to know she wasn't alone.

We ate the rest of our breakfast in silence before Zach rose and signalled to us that we'd better get started.

We set out like it was the first time, as though the night before hadn't counted. And how could it with darkness draped over everything? The beauty and vibrance of the rainforest were magical in the sunlight. There were two routes to the village, the trail we took the night before, which went up the volcano and around it, or a second that took us down toward the ocean and along the shore. Zach decided on the latter, which suited me perfectly as I was in a mood where I would rather drift slowly down a trail than have to climb up one.

A narrow trail, rarely used from the looks of it, branched off from the main trail and climbed up the ridge and toward the volcano at the centre of the island. Zach paused where the two trails connected and looked up into the vegetation. Chris quickly hoisted his camera onto his shoulder and took a few shots of the ocean, waves rolling toward the shore. He then turned and filmed the trees bending in the breeze, the ridges and hillsides, the mist rising up toward the volcano.

"There they are," Zach said.

Aldo was leading Joshua and Duncan down the ridge toward us. They weren't beaming like conquering heroes, so it seems we hadn't missed any earth-shaking discoveries.

Duncan avoided looking at me, knowing that I expected him to be the responsible one.

"You boys have fun?" I asked.

"It *was* a campfire," Joshua said. "The way it was positioned, near a hillside with plenty of tree cover, I couldn't clearly identify it with the infrared."

"Happens to the best of us," I said.

"I have returned your scientists safe and sound," Aldo said, smiling. He hooked his thumbs into his belt, arching his back slightly, as if calling attention to his well-developed pecs.

I saluted, pressing my fingertips to my temple, my palm facing down. "I was afraid I was dealing with a pair of deserters," I said. "Thanks for returning them."

"You're a long way from America," he said. "This is how it's done." He saluted me back, his palm facing outward.

"I've never understood the reason for the difference in salutes," I said.

"Well, I have to be getting back," he said. "Maybe we can discuss it in the commissary later." He then abruptly did an about-face and double-timed it back up the ridge. The route we had taken would have been easier, shorter and with level terrain, but I assumed he wanted the challenge. He was probably the type that did push-ups and pullups before appearing on camera, to appear more pumped up. Aldo had his commando reputation to uphold. He soon disappeared into the trees.

Joshua took his place at the front of the group, beside Zach, and we carried on down the trail toward the village.

Duncan walked beside me. He removed his Tilley hat and wiped his brow. "He was going regardless," he said quietly. "I thought it best that one of us go with him."

The "us" Duncan referred to were the people within the team dedicated to doing a skeptical science-based TV series. That was Saad, Duncan, me, and, I hoped, Lindsay. Danny's concern was ratings, and his idea of getting higher ratings was sensationalism and mystery. Joshua, whether he admitted it or not, came along to push his agenda, and Chris was here to film it all, regardless of what we found.

"I appreciate that," I said. "I wonder who was out here at that time of night?"

"Aldo was wondering the same thing. He suspects —"

"Drug runners?"

"What? No, no. Poachers," he said. "Or people looking to capture exotic animals and sell them as pets."

"I don't know which is worse," I said.

Duncan shrugged.

We carried on as one long procession. I was content to take it slow after my fall the night before. Maybe I had rushed headlong into situations too many times. Lindsay lingered behind us, seemingly lost in her own thoughts.

Danny's canteen was nearing empty as we approached the village, judging by the angle he had to tilt the thing to take another pull. He was slowing down, sweat beading on his forehead and visible in his close-cropped hair, like morning dew on a pristine lawn. Danny wasn't used to tropical locales, except those where you recline on a beach and sip fruity drinks.

"You're enjoying this, aren't you?" he asked me.

"It's an adventure," I said. "And I remember you complaining about my last choice of location, on account of it only having about two weeks of summer a year."

Saad looked back at us and smiled. I might have teased him in the past about wearing thermals on mild winter days and never being too far from a space heater, but the heat never slowed him down. Much of our summer was similar to the winter in Karachi, where he grew up.

"Do zombies count as cryptids?" Danny asked. "I could stand a trip to Haiti."

"Chupacabra," Chris said. "Puerto Rico is gorgeous, and I have family there."

At last, we traded the thick, sticky air of the rainforest for the exposed grasslands, the sun beating down on us with everything it had. Our proximity to the ocean provided some relief, with the breeze off the water chasing the humidity back into the jungle like wolves hunting deer.

Lindsay was no stranger to the cold, having grown up in Harbin and then moving to the northern U.S. Her tolerance to the heat, though, was about the same as mine. She trudged on silently, gripping the straps of her pack. Her long hair, which she'd allowed to return to its natural black after years of dyeing it, was braided today and stuck fast to the sweat on her back.

"Those are both good suggestions," I said. "But I was thinking we'd go after the yeti next. I doubt you'll have to complain about the heat in Nepal."

"There's always Loch Ness," Duncan said. "A lovely place to holiday if you're fond of fog, cold rain, and grey skies."

"Josh," Danny said, "What do you think, Puerto Rico or Nepal?"

"If it were up to me, I'd suggest we visit the Congo."

"M'kele M'bembe?" Duncan asked.

"Exactly!" Joshua said.

"Hmm," I said, "another jungle."

"You're supposed to be on my side," Danny said.

Zach slowed down as we approached a fork in the trail. He looked over his shoulder at us and pointed up the bisecting trail. "Up that way's where the research station is where they're studying those monkeys."

Lindsay glanced solemnly up the trail, then down at the dirt at her feet and kept right on. I walked a little faster and Saad matched my pace instinctively.

Duncan, Chris, Joshua, and even Danny knew to speed up, circling the wagons around Lindsay. The sooner we put some distance between that research station and our group, the better.

The village soon appeared in the distance, the thatched-roof buildings standing out amongst the greenery. In the foreground a dyke was visible, seemingly marking the borders of the village. As we came closer, we could clearly see that most of the structures were built several feet above the ground on stilts. The larger buildings had steps leading up into them, the smaller ones only ladders.

"Flooding is an issue in these low-lying areas," Zach explained. "Did you know that PNG is one of the ten most disaster-prone countries in the world?"

"Because of the flooding?" Saad asked.

"The rains and floods don't help," Zach said. "But the real trouble is earthquakes. The country sits on the collision point of several tectonic plates. It's part of the Ring of Fire. The heavy rains mixed with the earthquakes makes landslides a real killer."

The trail soon opened up onto a large avenue that ran through the centre of the village. The larger buildings were in the middle, with smaller residences seemingly in their orbit. On the grass between the buildings, several children kicked a soccer ball around, their mothers watching from the porches and openings in the wooden structures. Zach had explained that most of the men left the village during the day, mostly to fish, but also to travel into the highlands to gather wood and fruit.

There were two men in sight, however — the familiar faces of Gideon and Jacob. The pattern of biblical names wasn't lost on me. Joshua must have felt right at home. Our guides from the day before waved as we approached, placidly watching as we "explored" what they considered to be routine.

Gideon whistled and two of the children turned and came over. The boys, about ten and twelve, stood close to their father. The older of the two had more delicate features, a soft nose and prominent cheekbones. The younger one was stout little boy, the kind who looked destined to play football, or perhaps rugby in this part of the world. They stood in that pocket kids occupy, where they know to stand up straight and be seen, but don't expect any of the grown-ups to actually engage them.

Zach took off his blue-tinted sunglasses and rested them on his hat brim. Without the sunglasses, Zach looked like little more than a boy himself. His eyes told a different story, though. There was a something there that seemed very old, a kind of fatigue that appears in the faces of those who have lived through hard times. I'd seen that in my father's eyes. Zach broke the line we'd subconsciously formed, positioning himself in the middle of our group.

"Hey, Mikey, how are you, mate?" Zach asked the older boy.

The boy lit up the way kids do when an adult gets chummy with them. Zach, for his part, lit up, too. That look that I had just noticed seemed to disappear completely. He was having fun.

"Just brilliant, Zach," the boy said, smiling shyly.

"There's a lad," Zach said. "And how about you, little man?"

"Good," the other boy, who I now assumed was Joseph, said, stretching the word out the length of a breath.

"How about a high-five, Jo-Jo?" Zach asked, raising a palm.

Joseph planted his hand in that of our guide's, giving it a little push.

"All right," Zach said excitedly. "Can you take us to where you saw that light in the sky?"

The two boys almost tripped over each other as they peeled around their father and Jacob and ran toward the other end of the village. Gideon followed behind but Jacob stayed put. As the team began to follow, I heard Zach speaking to Jacob. "When we get back, they'll want to talk to Abraham."

As we followed the boys, I noticed an area away from the buildings where several women were tending to crops fenced off with barriers made from branches. I couldn't identify the crop from where I stood, but it was no surprise that subsistence farming was an integral part of survival in such a remote location.

On the farthest edge of the village, a network of trails led up into the highlands and toward the volcano, which stood over the island like a god; others meandered down to the coast.

The boys led us along a path that led us to the top of a bluff overlooking the water. Below, a flotilla of boats bobbed, as if conspiring to weigh down the water and hold it in place. I assumed they were local fishermen and made a note to ask Zach later.

The ground beneath us rose and fell like a sine wave as we tried to keep up with Michael and Joseph. The boys never looked back, and seemed to be in a race with each other to get to the spot where they'd filmed the glowing object that floated in the sky like jellyfish swim through water.

When I was their age, I'd wake up before my mother and head off into the woods behind our house, down into the ravine to the stream that ran through it. I'd follow it for hours. Sometimes Dad would track me through the pines and ferns, along the water's edge, not to scold me for wandering off by myself, but to join me in a shared solitude. I can't imagine letting my own child go off on her own over such rough terrain with no way of summoning help. For kids like Michael and Joseph, this island was their inheritance. They "played" along these trails, in the forest, and at the water's edge, and their adventures would directly translate into the skills they would need to carve out a life for themselves here.

The trail rose to a point that looked out over a forest, windswept palm trees acting as a natural marker between the beach and the lush green interior. There was no direct path down; only a trail that moved inland, then switched back, weaving along a hill and down toward the beach. I recognized this spot from the video, though in the daylight it had a great deal more depth and dimension. In the distance a river cut through the trees. It wasn't clearly visible from where we stood, except where it met and mixed with the ocean. The coastline was anything but smooth, marked with several coves and outcroppings of rock relentlessly pounded by waves, the white spray flying skyward.

"The video didn't show that river," Joshua said. "Is that the same one we were following last night?"

"I think so."

"That changes everything," he said.

"How so?" I asked.

"Now we know what it was doing here," he said. "Soaring down above this river to the coast, looking for fish, amphibians, insects, or crustaceans to eat. One sighting might have been a fluke, but now we know the creature returns to this spot, like any other predator would to a source of abundant food."

"Although pterosaurs *were* known to eat the creatures you mention, we cannot say for certain that they hunted like this, along rivers at night," Duncan noted.

"This is where the bioluminescence comes in," Joshua said excitedly. "The lights are the lure; the jaws are the snare."

The creationist was right about one thing. The river hadn't been visible in the video, and whatever that glowing object was, it seemed to be flying over the narrow channel of water. A drone seemed like the likeliest possibility, I thought, but then why would someone fly a drone over the river at night? And why come back again to the same spot? That's not the behaviour of macaque researchers. It seemed so unlikely that someone would travel to so remote an island to fly a drone around, especially if they weren't being funded by a major research organization to do so.

Joshua and Duncan continued to survey the landscape beside me while Chris, his camera set on a tripod, filmed it. Danny looked as though he couldn't care less. He sat back at the edge of some tall grass and finished the contents of his canteen.

"Does this trail connect with the one we took last night?" Lindsay, seemingly appearing from out of nowhere, asked Zach.

He glanced over his shoulder. "Right, yeah. It winds up the hill then meets the trail that runs alongside the river, where you'll find the site of Laura's famous wipeout."

"Ha ha," I said.

Lindsay brushed the hair back from her face, a few strands clinging stubbornly to her glasses. "Would you mind if we retraced our steps from last night? There were some limestone caves that I'd like to check out. If we're on the trail of a supposedly cave-dwelling creature, we should probably explore those caves."

My gut told me not to let her go. I wasn't comfortable with the team splitting up and going off without a guide, even though the trail was a familiar one. I was also worried about Lindsay. A man who had ruined her life, or at least a few years of it, was running around the island somewhere and I didn't want to risk them crossing paths again. On the other hand, if she felt the need to explore, to clear her mind, it might do her some good.

"I don't mind," I said, "but I don't want you going by yourself."

"I'll go," Danny offered. And with that, he rolled onto his back, did a couple of ab crunches, and jumped back to his feet.

I glanced over at Saad, who rolled his eyes at me. It was one of those instances where I knew he could read my mind. "I'll go, too," he said.

"Great," I said, before turning to Zach. "Are those caves safe?"

"As long as they don't go in too deep, they'll be fine," he said. "But I'm serious. It's okay to pop your head in, but don't go wandering."

Lindsay and Saad looked from Zach to me almost in unison like a pair of meerkats.

"Okay, you heard him, stay close to each other and don't go in too far," I scolded. "Get some footage of entering the cave, shoot as much as you can, but safely. We don't have any caving gear, so you're not equipped to do anything harder than what a casual tourist might try."

"You're the boss," Danny said, giving me a little wink.

Despite his attempt at being cute, I appreciated Danny in the role of chaperone. Nothing mattered to him more than the show, so I knew he wouldn't let any of us engage in reckless behaviour that might draw the ire of the network execs and harm the *Creature X* brand. Still, it was good that Saad was going along, too, to be the voice of reason and to actually care what happened, not just about his reputation and career.

"Remember where the trail around the caves splits off and comes back down to the village? Take it and meet us there," I said.

As the trio headed away up the trail that ran parallel to the edge of the bluff and the river then up the side of the volcano, we prepped the boys to do an interview on camera. They both seemed to know conversational English, but Zach stood by to catch the few stray words from their dialect. The boys described the night in question, setting the scene for when they saw the mysterious light hovering above the trees. Joshua and I stood by to ask questions.

"Ask them if the Ropen made any sounds," Joshua said.

"Ask them if whatever they saw made any sounds," I said. "We're not presuming this thing was a Ropen."

Zach smiled without looking at us, asking the boys about their sighting in a mishmash of Tok Pisin and English. The boys recounted their adventure, of running along these trails after dinner one night, then stopping at the point and looking out over the jungle and the ocean.

"Ask why they stopped at this particular spot," I said to Zach.

He put the question to the boys, who smiled shyly, eyes cutting semicircles in the grass and shrubs at their feet.

"We came to look for boats," Michael said.

The men from the village made much of their living fishing, but the fishing boats would have been in by that time, and they moored them closer to the village.

"Which boats?" I asked.

"We see a boat the night before, come along the beach," Michael said, making a swimming gesture with his right hand. "It turn up the river and go into the forest."

Zach looked at me quizzically. "Sounds weird, right?"

I nodded.

"We never see that boat before, we thought maybe it be back," the older of the two boys said.

"But instead, you saw that flying object?"

Michael waited for Zach to translate. "Yes," he answered.

"Thank you," I said.

Chris pulled away from the viewfinder and gave me a thumbs-up. Zach said it was time to get the boys home. After Chris had packed up his gear, we started back toward the village.

"What do you make of that boat the kids said they saw?" I asked Zach. "If it's unfamiliar to them, then it's probably not from the village or anywhere nearby."

"The locals use these rivers like roads to go deeper inland," he said. "But they don't take their fishing boats upstream, just outboards like the boat we used to come get you lot. The water is usually not deep enough for fishing boats, but after all that rain the other night, it might just have been manageable." Zach turned away and walked over to the edge of the bluff and looked down toward the river.

"If I had to guess, I'd say wildlife traffickers," he said. "PNG has more rainforest than almost any other country, only beat by the Amazon and the Congo Basin. The wildlife trade is a multimillion-dollar industry in this part of the world and the government doesn't have the resources to police it, on account of everything else on their plate. We're not so far out that it's difficult to get here by boat. And it's a piece of cake to sail up that river, fill up, then slip out again."

"What could they have been after?"

"Depends," Zach said, wiping his finger across his nose. "The locals pay big money for feathers from birds of paradise. It's PNG's national symbol, and its feathers are used in many traditional performances. One dead bird of paradise goes for forty dollars Australian. That's good money. If a hunter bags half a dozen in a day, he's set for months."

"That's awful! It is illegal to hunt them, though, right?"

"That's right, but it's a law that goes back to when PNG was a colony run by Australia. The usage of these feathers predates colonial rule."

"I guess it's easier to get away with it here than on the mainland."

"There's no police presence to speak of, only villagers who have bigger concerns than enforcing colonial laws," he said. "The other option could be international wildlife traffickers. Turtles are their cash crop. They might have just sailed up the river to conceal their boat and walked back to the beach. Sea turtles nest along there. Baby turtles bring in a pretty penny on the international market. They could fill a few sacks with baby turtles, then sail to Australia for a big payday."

"I guess if the money's right and it's low risk, you can't blame folks for trying to feed and clothe their families," I said, sighing.

"It's not a free lunch," Zach said. "These rivers are filled with crocodiles and even venomous catfish. Then on land there are the snakes, the spiders, and at least a half-dozen other critters likely to kill a person if they're not paying attention."

Zach was full of information about the inner workings of the island, its people, and the external forces at play upon it. But none of that was helping to identify the glowing aerial phenomenon from the video. It's possible that he had the answers and I wasn't asking the right questions, and that nagged at me as we walked back toward the village. If that was a drone, and it was tracking that boat, or monitoring that river for boat traffic, who was controlling it? Unlike the military-grade drones that carry out airstrikes, civilian drones have a limited range. Somebody must have been nearby, controlling the drone, but who?

EIGHT

The valleys and jungles of Papua New Guinea are known to hold a treasure trove of undiscovered and unclassified species of flora and fauna. Among them, suggest some, is the ropen, a winged reptilian creature that resembles — or perhaps is — a pterodactyl. Indeed, the ropen has become the flying hobby horse of creationists, who seek to find living dinosaurs as proof that the earth is far younger than evolutionary scientists lead the rest of the world to believe.

— Ishaan Tharoor, "Top 10 Famous Mysterious Monsters," *Time*, August 14, 2009

THE VILLAGE ELDER, ABRAHAM, WAS A DEVOUT Christian, a Baptist more specifically, and I noticed that he and Joshua got along swimmingly. They seemed to have the same opinions on modernity, women's clothing, music, movies, and TV and video games, although it was unclear if either had any expertise or experience with the subjects they discussed.

The stoop-shouldered Abraham clung to a walking stick that kept him upright. He looked as if he was dressed for work at Best Buy, in a blue golf shirt and tan khakis, but a white beard gave him the appearance of wisdom. The wrinkles around his eyes also helped with that.

Although he had a good command of English and spoke with clear Australian inflections, a younger man from Lab Lab, a village on the west coast of the island, stood with him. The man, who was addressed as "Cousin Tobias" by all, had come to stay for reasons that weren't entirely clear to me. His eyes passed over Duncan and me, then panned to Chris and Danny, who were discussing which microphone was best for the interview, ruling out the boom, then debating between the shotgun mic with parabolic attachment or a lavalier. The lav won out, and Danny clipped it to Abraham's blue shirt.

Chris set up the camera and had to interrupt the cordial conversation between Joshua and Abraham to get them back on task. Cousin Tobias stepped out of the frame but looked on, as if protecting the elder from any chicanery we might be planning. Joshua, Duncan, and I stood off camera, asking questions.

Abraham started with a story, not about something he'd witnessed, but something he'd heard as a small child that had stuck with him through the years. Apparently, before wooden caskets came into use, the dead bodies of Umboi Island residents were wrapped in leaves before they were buried. The smell of death, carried on the ocean winds up to the mountains, drew the Ropen out from its cave. The villagers would have to keep a watch over the burial plot for up to three nights after someone was interred, as the Ropen was known to raid fresh graves. Once wooden caskets were introduced, the Ropen no longer feasted on the dead.

"That's fascinating," I said. "Now can you tell us about your own encounter with the Ropen?"

"There were two," he said solemnly.

"I'd like to hear them both," I said.

"When I was a boy, my brother and I climbed up to the top of the mountain," he said, raising his hand, his index finger pointing toward the summit. "There's a lake there with water clear as air. You can see deep into the mountain. It was a long climb and we'd set out early in the morning, not arriving until the sun was in the middle of the sky. The trails weren't as well-worn then. We each had brought a sack of food and we spent the day swimming in the lake and eating on a flat floor made of rock.

"My brother was tired from the climb and the swimming and soon he fell asleep in the afternoon sun. It became dark as we climbed down. We had to move very slowly, very carefully. Then we saw a light in the distance, coming from over the sea, flying above our village and over the mountain."

"Can you describe the shape of what you saw?" Joshua asked.

Abraham shook his head. "I could only see light, a burning yellow, like the sun had left something behind, but smaller. My second encounter was at dusk. I saw it then."

"Describe that for us, please," I said.

As I turned to look at Chris, I noticed Danny and Saad making their way through the village. Lindsay was nowhere in sight.

"It was in the forest, not far from here," Abraham continued. "Luke — my brother — and I took a short-cut through a clearing. As we left the clearing and entered the forest, the closest tree to us seemed to move."

"The tree moved?" I asked, no longer focused on our subject, but on Danny and Saad.

Where was Lindsay?

"The trunk of the tree, it seemed to peel away. But it wasn't the bark, it was a creature, with leathery wings. It had wrapped itself around the tree trunk, but let go as we approached. It first fell to the ground, then flew up into the forest."

"Interesting," Duncan said, "that it couldn't fly from the tree trunk itself, but had to go to the ground before takeoff."

"How big would you say the creature was?" Joshua asked.

Abraham extended both of his arms out to his sides. "Twice as long as me," he said.

Duncan and Joshua started in on him with the questions about anatomical detail. Any fur? Scales? Did the creature have any digits on its wings, and if so, were they more like a pterosaur or a bat? The answers were less than satisfactory, as you'd expect from someone who'd had a shocking encounter decades earlier.

The experts took turns, no good cop/bad cop, just polite questioning that took Abraham at his word. The longer the interview continued, the less what Abraham described sounded like what Saad and I had seen through the forest canopy. Neither of us had enough data to compare notes. Aside from the size of the creature, there was only one attribute Abraham seemed sure of.

"Did you see the creature glow?" Joshua asked.

Abraham looked down at his fingertips as though he was counting on them. After a moment he looked back up. "Only the eyes," he said. "They glowed an awful red. It was like looking right into hell."

NINE

If they were going to be around, they're going to be somewhere where nobody's ever been, nobody's taken a camera, nobody's ever managed to capture an image. There aren't terribly many places left on the planet where that's the case. So, you would have to be going to the middle of the middle of the jungles of Brazil. The middle of the jungle of the Congo, or dare I say, maybe even some remote place like the mountain region of Papua New Guinea.

— Dr. David Martill, "Dr. Dave Martill & Pterosaurs," *Monster Talk*, October 12, 2009

DUNCAN, JOSHUA, AND CHRIS COULD HANDLE it from there. My priority was finding out where the hell Lindsay had gone. I was met with genuine surprise from Danny, who didn't seem to understand the gravity of the situation, or didn't care.

"You let her go off on her own?" I asked, annoyed.

"Oh, come on, it's just a short walk from the caves to the camp," Danny said dismissively.

"She wasn't feeling well," Saad said timidly. "She wanted to go back to camp."

Maybe she felt safer at the camp, or maybe she'd just lost the desire to carry on hunting cryptids. Both were understandable. I would never bench Lindsay, but if she wanted to stay on the sidelines, I felt I had to respect that.

"All right, let's wrap it up here and head back," I said.

The trail widened as we approached the camp. I stopped and listened to the distant chirps and howls from the jungle that surrounded us. Soreness competed with my sweat-covered skin for the prize of making me the most uncomfortable. I wasn't the only one in need of rest and a shower. Joshua and Duncan hobbled up the trail behind me, Danny and Chris behind them, like a platoon of soldiers returning from battle.

"I've never looked more forward to a cot in my life," Danny announced, veering toward the large tent where the men slept. "I'll say this for you, Laura, at least you picked a tropical location this time. I was getting pale as a ghost."

The men were eager to dump their packs in the tent and either sleep or head to the commissary for something to eat. The straps of my pack had made permanent tracks around my shoulders and I wanted nothing more than to take it off, lay down on my cot, throw something over my face, and drop off to sleep.

Across the camp, I saw Lindsay emerge from the commissary tent and walk toward me. I smiled, relieved she'd made it back safely.

"There you are," I said. "How were the caves?"

"They go deeper than I would have thought," she said. "I'd love to go back with proper gear."

That was the first time she seemed legitimately excited to be on the island.

"There might be time for that," I said. "But I need a little rest before we start shooting again tonight."

"Me, too," Lindsay said.

The scientists from the U.K. team were up at dawn, and for the most part stayed up until nightfall, so we expected we'd have the tent to ourselves. We had a few hours before we had to wake up for the night shoot.

I pushed the tent flap aside and walked in, several thoughts competing with the sensations of fatigue for my attention. The first thing I noticed was an odd smell, different from the thick dampness of the rainforest air. Then the flies. A sense of danger set off alarms in my brain. Then I saw him. I stopped dead in my tracks, gasped, and turned to push Lindsay back out the door. But I was too late. She stood there in the doorway, open-mouthed, looking as if she'd stepped on the third rail of a subway track.

It was Adam. He was lying on Lindsay's cot. On the ground beside him was my monogrammed Remington knife, the compact steel blade stained red with blood.

I knew he was dead.

Lindsay brought her fists to her face and staggered back. "Oh, fuck, no, Jesus, fuck …"

Religion and profanity came to everyone sooner or later. I took hold of her shoulders and guided her back outside. She kept looking over my shoulder, further etching that image into her mind.

"Saad!" I yelled the moment we were outside. I heard the panic in my voice.

The flap of the tent opposite whipped open and Saad emerged, his eyes locking onto mine. He ran over, scanning Lindsay for signs of injury then looking to me questioningly, his usual calm demeanor replaced by a resolute tension.

"Take her over there, now." I nodded toward a shady spot at the edge of the clearing.

"What's the big idea?" he asked.

It wasn't the time to criticize the lingo he'd picked up from old movies.

"There's a bloody dead body in our tent is what!"

"Another one?" he asked, incredulous, unable to help himself.

"Yeah, it's a fucking gift of mine, apparently."

I looked around, but aside from the three of us, nobody seemed aware anything was amiss. The U.K. team was going about their business, laughing and chatting and moving between the commissary and the lab.

I felt like I needed more time to think. I realized there was no explaining a corpse away. Especially one that had turned up on the cot of one of my team members, and more specifically, a team member who had a very clear motive for killing him. I thought she'd physically be able to do it, but I'd seen her reaction, and I knew she hadn't. Lindsay was capable and intelligent, and her attention to detail was unmatched. This was definitely not how she'd execute a premeditated murder. But a spur-of-the-moment thing … if he'd attacked her or said something that made her snap all of a sudden? I wasn't sure. I thought about my folding knife lying on the ground beside the body. That certainly didn't help matters any. God, even I could be a suspect. Almost everyone had seen me confront Adam the night before.

T E N

The creatures first came to the attention of missionaries who described these nocturnal fliers as having … razor-sharp teeth, muscular tearing claws and a very long whip-like tail with a split or flange on the end. There are reports from both investigators and natives of these creatures glowing in the dark.

— Terrence Aym, "Dinosaur Found
Alive: Two Species Recorded in Papua
New Guinea," Salem-News.com,
August, 12, 2010

DANNY HAD SETTLED INTO HIS COT, HIS EYES covered by a sleep mask, the logo of the Grand Papua Hotel printed across it on the bridge of his nose. The others reacted to my presence, but Danny didn't stir.

"Chris, Duncan, something awful has happened. I need you guys to come to our tent. Don't let anyone in or out."

"But —"

"Now! Please," I said to the cameraman.

Danny threw his legs over the side of his cot and sat up, peeling the sleep mask from his face. His expression was not a happy one. "What the hell's going on?!"

I ignored him. "Joshua, I need you to find Aldo and bring him to our tent, and be discreet."

He looked toward Danny.

"Don't look at him! Just do as I tell you. This is an emergency!"

He hopped to it, leaving Danny and I alone in the tent.

"Suppose you tell me what's going on," Danny said, yawning.

"You remember Adam … from last night?"

"Of course."

"Well, he's dead."

"Dead?"

"Yes, dead. It looks like maybe suicide. His body's in our tent."

"Damn."

"What's more, he's lying in Lindsay's cot."

"Well, that's just perfect."

"And one more thing …"

"Oh no. What?"

"It was my bloody knife that he used."

"This just gets better and better," Danny said, rubbing his eyes.

"We need to contact the embassy in Port Moresby," I said.

"Calm down. The network has a protocol in place for things like this."

"Well, can I assume it involves calling the goddamn embassy?"

"It certainly does," he said, bending down and rooting through a tote under his cot.

He looked up suddenly. "The phone's gone."

"What?"

"The satellite phone. It's not here." Danny continued to riffle through his things, moving from the tote to his backpack.

"Well, we have more than one," I said. "I'll get mine."

When I came out of the tent, I glanced over to the clearing. Lindsay was pacing back and forth, raking her fingers through her hair as Saad looked on, obviously concerned. Duncan and Chris were standing by the tent.

Joshua came across the camp, Aldo in tow. "What's all this, then?" Aldo asked.

"We have a body in our tent."

"You've got what?" he asked, too loud for my comfort.

I doubled down on using a quiet voice. "There's a body, Aldo. A dead man. In our tent."

"It's that bloody Yank, innit? Don't take a fortune teller to know that one was trouble."

Aldo's victim-blaming needed to be explored, as well as how he was so sure that it was Adam in there, but that had to wait. He was no stranger to ugly situations and he knew the camp and the U.K. crew better than anyone on my team. He was also more likely to know what to do.

"All right then, let's have a look," he said, heading toward the tent.

"There's one more thing," I said.

He stopped and narrowed his eyes at me.

"Danny's sat phone is missing. There's another one in the tent with my things, I just thought you should know. It's peculiar that Danny's is missing. There isn't a person on the planet more attached to his phone than Danny LeDoux, and he isn't likely to misplace it."

"Not to worry, we have our own," he said. "We'll call in the PNG authorities. Let's just see what we're dealing with first."

"I want to limit how many people go in and out of there," I said. "But I'm going in to look for my phone."

"That's fine," Aldo said. "Keep your people outside. Just you and I will go in."

Duncan looked around as he stepped aside to let us in. We hadn't managed to attract much attention so far. The U.K. team was using the daylight as best they could, not wasting a moment as their expedition rapidly drew to a close.

Aldo stepped into the tent with a soldier's bearing, the way I imagined he had moved into tents on a base in Kandahar. He looked left and right, then zeroed in on the body and moved quickly toward it, mindful of his surroundings and his foot placement.

He stood at the foot of the cot, observing the same things Lindsay and I had. Adam's body sunk into the cot, his right arm hanging over the side, his wrist slit, a dark stain below it on the ground. Beside the cot was the knife, sticky with blood.

I didn't worry about the body much the second time around. I slid my satchel from beneath my cot and unzipped the pocket where I kept the satellite phone. Unlike Danny, who kept his with other equipment and valuable items, I left mine with the essentials, where I could grab it in a hurry and always have it close. But the phone wasn't there.

"My sat phone's gone, too," I said, turning to Aldo. There was a hiccup in my mind, a glitch, where I suddenly asked myself, why am I trusting this guy? Is it because his military bearing reminds me so much of my father?

"This man killed himself," Aldo said.

"It sure looks that way."

"Meaning?"

"Meaning it sure looks that way," I repeated. "Maybe if we search his pockets, we'll find a note. It's just …"

"It's just what?"

"It just doesn't feel right," I said. "We find a body, we want to call it in, then our sat phones are just … gone?"

"Looks like this nutter offed himself, either feeling guilty about doing your friend wrong or 'cause he wanted to hurt her more. I don't see that the phones are related."

We stood there in silence, the two of us, or three of us, depending how you saw it. I checked my satchel again, as if there was any way I could have missed the sat phone in the first go-round.

Aldo made a quiet growling sound. "All right, no more messing about," he said. "I'm going to get my phone. You stay here. We'll keep this quiet until we can communicate with the outside world. Don't want a bloody panic on our hands."

He looked down at the radio clipped to my belt. "Go to channel six. Radio in if there's a problem, but I won't be more than a minute or two."

Aldo left, parting the flaps just enough to get his broad frame through then pulling them closed behind himself. He was a careful man, resolute in his actions. Was my dad like that? Was he so focused every time he left Mom and me to seek out Bigfoot, or the Minnesota dogman, or thunderbirds in the southwest? And if he was, why was he not resolved to come back home?

The pull of the body, like its own gravity, yanked me from my thoughts. I was caught in its orbit, even when my back was turned, keenly aware of its position, of its hold on me. Death has its own gravity.

"You fucking asshole," I muttered.

He had ruined Lindsay's pursuit of her doctorate, and now he may have ruined her second chance. I knew it was bad form to speak ill of the dead, but in that moment I couldn't care less. There are some men who think they are the centre of the universe and accept nothing less, even in death.

I looked at the blood that had pooled beneath the cot, a darker shade than ruby. Crimson maybe. I walked closer, but was careful not to contaminate the scene. I ran through all the mortises in my head. *Pallor mortis*, the onset of paleness in the skin as the blood stops flowing is the first sign. That begins the moment the heart stops. His eyes looked glassy, but hadn't clouded over yet, which happens when the potassium in the blood cells breaks down. That process usually occurs in the first three hours after death, so Adam hadn't been dead very long. The pupils dilate during *rigor mortis*, but that hadn't happened here. His pupils were tiny dots in a sea of grey blue, almost invisible from where I stood. Pupil myosis was unexpected, but I'm no coroner. There was a stain on his shirt, I noticed, the little specks the colour of dough.

My cellphone was in the duffel bag beneath my cot, untouched by the sea of blood on the ground. I took it out and took several photos of the scene, then recorded a short video. Someone might want to see the scene as we found it, or we might need to prove it looked a certain way. Or maybe I was just being paranoid. With my knack for stumbling over dead bodies, it seemed like a reasonable precaution.

Suddenly, I was gripped by an urge to search the body. I knew I shouldn't disturb the scene any more than I already had. Even if a proper investigation wasn't conducted, I could lose my job if I was seen as perverting the course of justice. But in that moment, I felt like I owed it to Lindsay to understand what happened as best I could.

Lightly patting his pockets, I tried to stay as far from

the body as I could and not to touch his belt buckle, watch, or any other surface from where a fingerprint could be lifted.

He seemed to have nothing in his pockets. Had he made the walk here with no water bottle? Was that odd or did it make sense that he wouldn't be concerned with keeping hydrated? Or did he drop it somewhere? And what about the knife? It was definitely mine, the wood-handled Remington my dad had given me for my sixteenth birthday. I'd left it in my bag, beneath the cot. Had he set out to kill himself in Lindsay's bed, wouldn't he have brought a knife with him instead of leaving it to chance? It was damn near impossible to put yourself in the head of someone so distraught that they would slice open their wrists and let their life drain out onto the ground. I read somewhere that people who commit suicide naked are the ones who really mean it. They don't care about being discovered since they plan to be dead before that happens. Maybe coming with just the clothes on his back was the equivalent to being naked. He was not prepared for anything past his final act.

"Laura, do you read me?" Aldo's voice came over in a hushed tone.

"I'm here," I said, the two-way radio in one hand, my cell in the other.

"My sat phone's missing, too. I can't find the others, either. I'm going to have another look around without causing a panic. I'll be back with you shortly."

"Copy that," I said.

I looked down at Adam's forearm, his watch hiked up about two inches from the fatal gash. A wristwatch, though somewhat odd in an age where everyone had a cellphone, made sense for a researcher on an island where his phone was mostly useless. But did people keep their watches on when they slit their wrists?

Kneeling down beside the cot, I looked at the watch face. There was a crack across the glass. I had to lean in very close to read the time, precariously holding myself over the pooling blood. The watch had stopped about two hours earlier. Could he have hit it that hard on the edge of the cot?

Suddenly, I heard voices outside the tent, the sound of one person being curt with two others trying to be exceedingly polite. I knew who it was before I turned to see Celine push her way past Duncan and into the tent. She entered with the air of someone in control, a queen surveying her kingdom. Her mask of superiority cracked once her eyes landed on Adam.

"Jesus Christ!" she yelled, bringing her hands up to her face but not quite touching it.

"It's okay, Celine," I said and took a step toward her.

She put her hands out like I might attack her. "It's certainly not okay!"

"Let's step outside," I said, pointing toward the exit.

"Stop talking to me like I'm a bloody idiot!" She pushed past me and stood over Adam. "What have you done? Dear lord, what have you done?"

Duncan poked his head in.

"Go find Aldo, tell him the cat's out of the bag," I whispered. I turned back to Celine, who stood with arms crossed, gripping her elbows tightly. "Celine, I ..."

She looked up with something between anger and hatred in her eyes. "This is *your* fault! You brought that stupid girl here, and for what? To find a bloody dinosaur! Of all the idiotic notions. It's bad enough Lindsay ruined Adam's career! He was just turning a corner and —"

It didn't seem like the right time to correct her about the point of pterosaurs being dinosaurs — they weren't. But my own anger was starting to rear its ugly head and I balled my hands into fists to contain it. "You're upset, you've suffered a shock. Say any stupid thing that comes to mind, if that makes you feel better. But get it out of your system now."

She turned to me, the emotion draining from her face. The burning anger was gone and it sent a chill down my spine. She closed the distance between us and I slid my right foot back to get into a stable stance, not knowing if she was going to cuss me out or take a swing at me. "Everything was fine before you brought *her* here," Celine said, bumping me with her shoulder on the way out.

We both knew who the "her" was. I thought I was doing Lindsay a favour, giving her a job, the kind of favour I would want done for me. It turns out that I had just made her life so much worse.

Aldo and Celine narrowly avoided crashing into each other as he rushed into the tent. He instinctively tried taking her by the shoulders but she weaved out of his grasp with an impressive display of reflexes and footwork.

"I'm getting Dr. McTavish," she declared.

I watched her storm away. We needed to get all our ducks in a row before Celine raised hell. Aldo decided to follow her and I turned to Duncan. "Can you watch the tent and keep an eye on Lindsay at the same time?"

"I don't see why not," he said.

"Saad," I yelled over to him. "Let's go talk to Danny. He says the network has a contingency plan for this. Let's find out what that is."

He and I crossed the gulf between the tents, but I stopped short. "I'm sorry I took that tone with you, Saad."

"I shouldn't have said anything ..."

"Still," I said.

Danny was sitting on his cot, his glasses in one hand. He pinched the bridge of his nose with the other. "Tell me you have some good news."

"My phone was in my satchel, but it was gone by the time we found the body, which means that someone planned this ahead of time."

"Or you could have just lost your phone," Danny said. "That does happen."

"Are you listening to yourself? You think we both just happened to lose our satellite phones?"

"You're the one who dismisses seemingly supernatural occurrences as coincidence on a regular basis."

"Well, I wouldn't say —"

"Quiet, Saad."

"No, you be quiet, Danny! Try listening more than you talk, for once," I snapped. "I know that's asking a lot."

"What's asking a lot is you expecting me to believe that Adam whatever-his-name-is snuck into our camp, stole our satellite phones, then offed himself. Why would he do that?"

"Maybe he wanted to hurt Lindsay," I said. "Given their history, I wouldn't eliminate the possibility that he wanted to control her, to make her suffer in his own way. Why else kill himself on her cot? Maybe he thought just calling in the police from the mainland and having his body removed and sent to the embassy would be too easy. He wanted to make a big deal out of his last act."

"You hardly knew the man," Danny said.

"You're right, this is all supposition," I said.

"Not a theory, but a hypothesis," Danny said, using my words against me.

"There is another possibility," I said.

"Which is?"

"Adam didn't kill himself at all."

"Please don't go there. Don't say it, let's just forget —"

"You think it was murder?" Saad asked.

"Don't encourage her, Saad!"

"Don't you talk down to him, Danny," I said.

"Why? That's your exclusive domain?"

I raised a fist. "Danny, you're dangerously close to —"

"Both of you, stop acting like assholes!" Saad shouted.

Danny froze like an ice sculpture; I felt like a deer in the headlights.

Saad stood, chest rising as he filled his lungs with air. The skin of his cheeks was flushed red. "I'm sorry," he said finally, letting out a deep breath.

"No, I'm sorry. You're right," I said.

I looked at Danny. He shrugged. It was enough. We continued.

"I'm not saying it's definitely murder, I'm not saying it was suicide, all I know is that a man is dead and our satellite phones are missing, and these circumstances, when put together, are pretty damn strange."

Danny threw his head back and looked up at the ceiling.

"Aldo can't find his phone, either. He's looking for the others they brought, but he was striking out last we spoke. This goes beyond just the two of us."

Dr. McTavish suddenly burst into the tent, red-faced and breathing hard. He looked at us wide-eyed, trying to overcome his shock enough to get a sentence out. My team remained silent as we awaited the Scottish scientist to get his hard-fought thoughts out. "What in holy hell is going on around here?" he said finally.

I stayed quiet, not sure if he was really expecting an answer to so broad a question.

"There's a dead man in the ladies' tent," Saad said quietly.

"And all our satellite phones have disappeared," I added.

McTavish put his hands on his hips and stared up at the ceiling. "I should have known better than to let you Bigfoot people join my expedition," he said.

"I doubt you had a say in it," Danny said. "And we're hardly 'Bigfoot people.' My team are researchers, just like yours."

McTavish's eyes grew even wider as he glared at Danny, redness overtaking his entire face.

"We have to contact the mainland," I said.

"I'll use my satellite phone," McTavish said.

"Are you sure you still have it? Ours are missing. So is Aldo's."

"I'm sure," he said.

McTavish reached into the cargo pocket in the side of his right pant leg, removing the phone. I felt the tension leaving my upper back and shoulders. Saad let out a long sigh. Danny shot me something of an I-told-you-so or see-you-were-overreacting look that I would have loved to slap from his face. But the moment was fleeting.

"Hold on, what's this then?" McTavish said. He stabbed the keypad with his index finger, then used his thumb to press the button on the side. He tried several times, then pressed it one last time, holding it down for the count of ten. He then turned the phone around in his hands, slipping the back plate off. "Bloody hell," he said. "This is a fresh battery. I don't understand what's going on here."

"Give it here," Danny said, impatient as always.

The scientist handed the phone over. For Danny, electronic devices like phones and tablets are just extensions of his body. It's like his superpower. But he'd finally found his kryptonite. Saad, being fairly tech-savvy, leaned in. He looked at me and shook his head.

Just then, Aldo came in, with Zach right behind him.

"It's as bad as we thought," I said. "No sat phones."

Aldo turned and looked at Zach.

"Don't look at me, mate. I use your spare. I don't carry one on me under normal circumstances."

"There's nothing normal about these circumstances," I said, which was an I-told-you-so of my own.

"I'll pop down into the village and use their radio. It's closer than Opai Beach and there aren't many people on this part of the island," Zach said. "I shouldn't be gone more than a few hours."

Danny looked me, and I looked from him to Saad, then to Aldo, like our glances were a hot potato.

"We should all go," I said. "At least, my team and Aldo."

"How do you figure that?" Danny asked.

"We have one dead body already," I said. "Safety in numbers. Dr. McTavish, we'll tell everyone what happened and that the ladies' tent is off limits. Keep your people close."

He closed his eyes, tucking in his chin like he was praying before giving a little nod.

"We'll head down to the village," I continued. "Zach, you take Danny and the others to use the radio. Aldo, Saad, and I will split off and find Adam's colleague. He deserves to know what happened. He's also likely to have a satellite phone or a radio, so we can explore that avenue, too. All our bases will be covered and we'll all be safer until help arrives."

"The wanker did himself in," Aldo said. "I don't think the rest of us are in any danger. We need to find where he put all the sat phones. It can't be far. There's a chance we can find them and get a message out."

"I don't think he killed himself," I said. "It looks that way, sure, but I think someone deliberately set it up to look that way."

"Why would you think that?" McTavish asked, looking at me as though I had two heads.

"His wrists were slashed with my knife," I said, "so are we supposed to believe he came all the way here and snuck into camp to kill himself, but didn't bring something with which to do the deed?"

"Maybe he just came to talk with Lindsay and got tired of waiting," Aldo said. "He was in there, so he riffled through your things, found the knife, then decided it was all 'goodbye, cruel world.'"

"I've considered that possibility," I said. "But there are still some things that bother me."

"Like what?" Danny asked.

"His broken watch, for one. That didn't happen lying on the cot. I think he fell somewhere else, broke the watch, then was brought there."

"He died right there," Aldo said. "You can tell by all the blood on the ground."

"You're right," I said. "But I figure maybe he was drugged, then dragged up here, set down in the cot, then killed."

Danny rolled his eyes. Zach, Aldo, and McTavish just looked confused. Saad was doing the math in his head. If nothing else, I could at least count on him to hear me out and consider what I was saying.

"That seems far-fetched," Saad said after a moment.

Et tu, Saad?

"I agree," I said. "I'd be more inclined to doubt it were it not for the missing phones. If someone was able to steal or sabotage all of our phones, then they know the camp well enough, and our routines, to pull something like this off. Adam couldn't have done this. I know he was here visiting Celine, but to know the whereabouts of all of your phones, and ours? How could he have?"

"There are easier ways to kill a man," Aldo said.

"Murder isn't always the endgame," I said. "Sometimes it's just one play in a series of plays."

The tent flaps were torn open and Celine came in. The men cleared a path for her. She was aglow with fury. "Dr. McTavish, I demand to know what's going on here!"

Bewildered, he turned to her, looking her up and down as though she'd just appeared in a puff of smoke. "If I knew that, my dear, I'd certainly tell you."

"We should get moving," I said to Zach.

"Where are you going?" Celine snapped, focusing all her fury on me.

"We need to call for help," I said.

"You don't need to go anywhere for that," she said before turning to McTavish. "Why are they trying to leave?" Her anger was beginning to give way to something else. Tears formed in her eyes. "I don't understand!

Adam's dead and they're trying to leave! She threatened him! Just last night!"

Dr. McTavish raised an eyebrow.

"At the party," I said. "I told him to stay away from Lindsay, or I'd make him regret it. I didn't threaten to kill him or anything like that."

Aldo closed the distance and put his hands on Celine's shoulders, tilting his head down to look her in the eye. "We have no phones, no means to communicate with the mainland. I'm going with them. We won't be long. We just have to find a way to call for help."

She closed her eyes and nodded, trying to stifle the swell of feelings. "No phones?" she said after a pause.

It was Aldo's turn to nod.

"How can that be?" Celine asked. "What's happening?"

It was the question on the marquee in all of our heads, but none of us had the answer.

"We should be searching the camp, the phones have to be around here somewhere," she said. "Nobody should be going anywhere. How do we know that you haven't stashed the phones away in your gear? You could be taking them out of the camp. How do we know you're coming back?"

Maybe it was grief or shock, but Celine was sounding paranoid. But maybe she had a point. I don't mean could one of my team have stolen the phones and killed Adam — I didn't think any of us knew where the U.K. team even stored their satellite phones. But should we maybe round up every member of both teams, keep them in the commissary, search their bags?

"Is your entire team on-site?" I asked Dr. McTavish.

"What? Oh yes, I believe so."

"Brodie isn't here," Aldo said.

"He's off in a blind, looking for pygmy parrots to film," Dr. McTavish said.

"We should gather everyone," I said, "explain the situation, and try to keep everyone close, either in the commissary, the cataloguing station, or both. Until we know what's going on, or until we can get help."

I looked at Celine. "And feel free to search our packs before my team heads out, if it will make you feel better," I said.

"I don't think that will be —"

Dr. McTavish was cut short by a sharp glance from Celine. It took a second for him to recover his train of thought. "Aye, we'll have a look in your packs, just to set everyone's minds at ease."

I nodded.

"That's fair," Aldo said, before gently guiding Celine outside of the tent.

The rest of us followed. Saad joined Lindsay, Chris, and Duncan outside the tent. Joshua stood alone nearby. McTavish took Celine by the elbow and escorted her toward the commissary.

McTavish suddenly stopped and looked back at us. He paused, then sent Celine on alone by pressing her shoulder gently. He came back and stood facing Aldo. "What about the helicopter?"

McTavish had mentioned it earlier. A small number of the U.K. team were taking a helicopter to a nearby island to spend the day cataloguing butterfly species. The U.K. team was leaving at dawn to hike toward the nearest airfield where the helicopter would be fueled and waiting.

"It'll be no use to us," Aldo said. "We need to get a message out before it arrives."

"But will you be back in time?" McTavish asked.

"If not, go without me. But be sure to take Celine. It would do her good to get her away from all this."

It felt like a dream had turned rapidly into a nightmare and there was no waking up. I had to round up the others and get our trip to the village underway. The rest of the team were watching me from the moment I left the tent, but I had no answers for them. They continued watching me as I approached.

"Give us a second, guys," I said.

Duncan, Joshua, and Chris joined Danny, Aldo, Zach, and Saad by the men's tent.

Lindsay looked up as I approached. Although she didn't say a word, I saw her back stiffen, her jaw clench, the muscles of her shoulders tense up. I stepped closer and hugged her. After a second, she hugged me back. Then she started to cry. I could feel all the tension in her body flowing out into the jungle air. I was tempted to let it all go, too, but the unfamiliar territory and prying eyes reminded me I had to keep it together.

"What ... is ... h-happening?" Lindsay asked between sobs.

"I wish I could tell you," I said quietly.

"Did he kill himself?"

"That's what it looks like," I said.

She peeled away from me, looking me in the eye. "Did you find a note?"

I shook my head.

"But you looked, right? I know you looked! I know you!"

"I looked," I said, "but there was nothing there. It could be on his phone, maybe on a computer back at the research station. I don't —"

"Adam would have left a note! You don't know him! If he did this, he'd have made sure we knew. He would have made sure *I* knew! He'd have played the martyr."

Lindsay brought her hands up to her face, then wiped her eyes and cheeks with her fingertips. "I'm sorry. I must sound like such a bitch."

"Don't apologize," I said. "I was thinking the same thing. If he had something to say to you, why not say it?"

I didn't answer my own question out loud, but it occurred to me the moment I said it that not leaving a note might cause Lindsay to torture herself with the uncertainty of it. Adam put her through hell once with his mind games, might he not try to do so again?

"Listen to me, I'm not going to let this touch you, understand me? We'll figure this out," I said. "But now it's my turn to sound like a bitch. Did you go in the tent before the rest of us came back?"

"What? Of course not."

"I had to ask, I'm sorry. If someone claims later that they saw you going in there, now I'll know they're lying."

The other possibility was that it was murder, meant to look like a suicide. It certainly appeared that way to me. But it was a superficial set-up. If my hunch was correct, a toxicology screen would show that he was drugged. I wondered if his fingerprints were even on my knife? Whoever could have done this knew about Adam's history with Lindsay, and knowing that, didn't want to risk that she could potentially identify his handwriting, so a forged note was too great a risk.

"We have to get moving," I said.

"What? Where are we going?"

"Back to the village, to call for help."

She looked lost, her brown, tear-filled eyes searching my face for answers. "I don't understand," she said. "Can't we call from here?"

"Nobody can find a satellite phone," I said.

Fear, confusion, frustration, they all appeared on her face in some form. They were lingering beneath the surface in me, too, but I kept my game face on for Lindsay.

I heard the sound of footsteps approaching and turned.

"I'm sorry," Danny said, with uncharacteristic kindness, "but we'd better get going. I've asked Chris and Joshua to stay here, if for no other reason than to placate any local law enforcement that might accuse us all of leaving the scene."

Maybe Danny meant that. But in the back of my mind, I suspected that he didn't want to leave company property unattended. Whatever his reasons, it didn't really matter. I'd have asked for Lindsay to stay if I thought the rest would be better for her. But how could she rest knowing what was so close by?

ELEVEN

As Western missionaries began to pene-
trate the deep jungles and remote islands
of PNG, stories of a flying creature called
the Ropen ("demon flyer") began to be reported. Described as a nocturnal creature,
the Ropen possesses two leathery wings
like a bat with "hands" on each wing, a
long tail with a diamond-shaped flange on
the end, and a prominent beak. The creature is thought to still inhabit the islands
of New Britain and Umboi, located in the
Bismarck Archipelago. The Ropen is said
to have a taste for decaying flesh. Reports
of harassment at native funeral gatherings
at the government station of LabLab (on
Umboi), and other attempts to disinter
corpses suggests that the Ropen is a carrion
animal. PNG natives will even put tin roofs
over fresh graves to deter the creature.

— David Woetzel, "The Fiery Flying
Serpent," *Creation Research Society
Quarterly* 4, no. 42 (March 2006)

SAAD STAYED WITH LINDSAY AS I FILLED UP
canteens for the three of us, grabbing granola bars and
fruit from the commissary for the road. It didn't take
long, a minute or two, but the eyes of the U.K. team,
tracking my every move, made it seem much longer.
Before we were just curiosities, not real scientists. But
we had become the proverbial albatross.

I walked back quickly to the others, all eager to get
out of the camp and contact the authorities. Zach led
the way without his usual smile or small talk. We knew
the way to the village by then, so we didn't need him
to guide us there, but we needed him to speak to the
villagers, to be the familiar face.

Aldo hung back, which seemed out of character for
him, from what I had witnessed so far. He was a leader,
not a follower. Zach did seem to grate on him, but I
wondered, too, if he wanted to keep an eye on us. He
didn't seem to buy that Adam didn't commit suicide, but
maybe he didn't want to reveal what he really suspected.

The walk was mostly downhill, which was a bless-
ing. The humidity had a tangible thickness to it, like
walking through cobweb after cobweb. We needed
a moment to rest, but that moment refused to come.
Our procession moved through the rainforest quietly,

only the sound of the ocean as we approached the coast broke the silence.

When we came to a fork in the trail, Duncan, Lindsay, and Danny followed Zach toward the village. Saad, Aldo, and I split off to the left, taking the smaller trail, which took us away from the coastline.

Despite their name, crab-eating macaques had a varied diet. Still, the research station was situated just a short hike from the ocean. One of the attributes that make crab-eating macaques so destructive to the habitats they invade is their omnivorous and not overly specialized diet. They devastate local bird populations by consuming their eggs, change plant distributions in their new habitats by voraciously eating certain fruits and scattering their seeds far and wide, and enter quickly into synanthropic lifestyles with local human populations.

These macaques, which were quite cute when their mouths were shut but downright sinister when they smiled, lived in social groups of up to eight adults, and were governed by the females of the population. Males were exiled from the group once they reached puberty, which I imagined was good for orderly group dynamics but terrible for the young males' socialization skills. The species was also known as long-tailed macaques, which must have led to confusion with lion-tailed macaques, by either young primatology students or autocorrect.

The research station was a small wooden structure about the size of a double-wide trailer, built on short stilts on the side of a hill. The flag of the International

Wildlife and Sustainability Foundation, which was white with a green globe in the centre with roots growing beneath it, flew in the ocean breeze from a small pole above the door. The branch of an acacia tree stretched over top of it. All other vegetation seemed to have been cleared away to give the occupants a good vantage point from the structure's windows.

As the three of us approached the station, following the trail that overshot the structure slightly then hooked back, the door opened. The occupant kept half his body concealed and looked at us suspiciously. "G'day," he said.

He looked to be in his midthirties and wore a blue cotton T-shirt, sweat stains visible under his arms and around his neckline, and a pair of khaki shorts. He had on a tan-coloured baseball cap that read "Murray's Craft Brewing."

"Hi there," I said, closing the gap between us. "My name is Laura Reagan."

"The TV personality," he said, as though he recognized my name from a dossier somewhere.

"You could say that."

"My name's Busby," the man said.

"This is Saad Javed, and you may already know Aldo Middleton."

"More TV personalities," the man said.

I ignored those statements of fact. "We have some bad news," I said.

"Come inside," he said, backing into the research station, letting the door creak wide open.

Inside was spare and neatly organized. There were two bunks toward the rear of the building. A built-in ledge under the front windows served as a desk for the researchers. The two workstations provided accurate character studies of the two men. One was neat, with pens in a cup, notebooks stacked beside a laptop, IWSF stationary, a pair of binoculars in a leather case against the wall. The other looked like the after photo of the first one being struck by a typhoon: notebooks scattered all over it, pens and highlighters thrown willy-nilly, scraps of paper covered in scribbles forming a patchwork like a quilt over the desk.

Beneath the ledge, several totes were stowed against the wall. There was a shelf to my right with everything you'd expect to find in such a place — a solar power cell for charging laptops and other devices, a first aid kit, a flare gun, a video camera, another pair of binoculars, and a couple of two-way radios. There was a short-wave radio on the ledge between the workstation and the kitchenette area, a section of ledge with a kerosene stove and some MREs.

"So, what's this about bad news?" he asked. "I don't think I need any more today."

"Your colleague, Adam, is dead," I said bluntly.

"What? How?"

"Apparent suicide," I said.

"Why do you say 'apparent'?"

"It looks as though he snuck into a tent in our camp and slit his wrists," I said.

"Good god." Busby brought his hand up to his

mouth, his thumb and forefinger drawing a circle around its edges. He stared off at something in the corner. The news we'd given him was registering like a webpage that just wouldn't load.

"This would have been within the last three hours, we think. How was he behaving this morning?"

He jerked his head up quickly, looking me in the eye. "Business as usual. We made our early morning observations. Adam stayed with the troop. I came back here, made a report, and radioed in." He pointed toward the radio.

"Can you radio for help?" I asked. "Our satellite phones are missing and we need to report this. We've sent part of our team on to the village to look for a phone, but you probably have protocols in place should something happen to one of you."

Busby raised an eyebrow. "That's the other bit of bad news," he said. "My radio's out. It was functioning perfectly this morning, now I can't seem to power the damn thing up."

"Where's your sat phone?" Aldo asked.

Busby walked across the room to one of the totes tucked under the wooden ledge. He slid it out, undoing the clasps and opening it wide like a treasure chest. He removed a smaller black case and opened it.

"I'll be …" he said.

Saad looked at me, and I passed the glance on to Aldo. Hot potato round 2.

"It seems like someone has been training your macaques to steal satellite phones," I said.

Busby closed the black case and put it back into the tote. "I want to see the body," he said. "Take me to it."

How quickly his fellow primatologist had become "it."

"We need to call it in first," Aldo said.

"You said you have some colleagues on their way to the village, right? I want to see the body now."

Losing a colleague and friend is a trauma, undoubtedly, and trauma can make you act strange. But was there more to it than that?

"I can show you pictures," I said, taking the phone out of my pocket.

"You photographed the scene?" Busby asked.

"I assumed it would take a while before the authorities could get to our camp; I wanted to be able to show them the scene exactly as we had found it."

"Good thinking." Busby reached out his hand and I gave him my phone, the gallery of morbid pictures opened on the screen. He swiped through them slowly, lingering over some longer than others. He then watched the video I had taken. "The close-ups of the eyes and the watch were smart," he said to me. "I still need to see the body, though. And the sooner the better."

Aldo nodded. "I'll take him back to camp. You two rendezvous with the rest of your group. We're not far from the village."

Aldo telling me what to do rubbed me the wrong way, but it was my chance to show that I could keep my nose clean. Let the dead body be someone else's problem this time. I already had two under my belt. Unclipping the radio from the strap of my pack, I called Danny.

"Danny, it's Laura, are you reading me?"

His voice came through as though he was just a few feet away. "Yeah, loud and clear."

"Saad and I are heading your way. Any luck finding a satellite phone or shortwave radio in the village?"

"No one's here."

"What?"

"It's a ghost town," Danny said.

"Okay," I said. "We're coming to you, over and out."

The longer the day went on, the less anything made sense. It was prime fishing time, so a large number of villagers were likely out in their boats, but the whole village? That made no sense. Where were the children? Where were the elderly?

"That's weird," Busby said. He took a step back and leaned against the counter.

"That's not normal," Aldo said, as if he hadn't heard Busby a half-second earlier.

"Let's stick to the plan, and be quick about it," I said. "This doesn't feel right at all. We need to call for help then get back to camp."

"Agreed," Aldo said.

Saad nodded and Busby pushed off the counter. I couldn't be sure, but as he did so, it looked as if he slid something — a phone maybe? — into his pocket. Then he grabbed his pack from one of the two hooks on the back of the door and stuffed a water bottle, a camera, and some other things in. Aldo was the first out the door, with Saad and I in tow.

Busby came out last. He pulled the door shut behind him and looked the opposite way we'd come. "There's a trail we can take up over that ridge," he said to Aldo. "It'll shave twenty minutes off our journey."

Suddenly, there was a loud crack that echoed through the forest. Busby fell back against the door. Three more shots ripped through the air and tore into the wooden planks of the research station. I pushed Saad down into the dirt as a bullet lodged in the wood just above my head, splinters flying.

"Move, move, move!" Aldo called out.

Saad rolled under the station for cover. Aldo ducked down in the other direction. I scrambled to my knees and opened the door to the station. As more bullets hit the side of the structure, I grabbed Busby's arm and dragged him inside. A trail of blood smeared across the floor. He cried out the harder I pulled.

Aldo ran through the door, tackling me as another volley of bullets flew through the air and chewed up the inside of the research station. Once we'd both hit the deck, we took hold of Busby and pulled him deeper inside. The three of us huddled there on the floor, near the workstations, the door left wide open.

"Get ... the lock ... box," Busby said, struggling with each syllable. He gestured at one of the totes with his nose.

Aldo reached over and slid the tote across the floor. I crouched and half ran to the shelf where I'd seen the first aid kit, pulling it down quickly. The tin box marked *flare gun* fell down and landed near my feet. I kicked it back toward Busby and Aldo as I dropped back into a crouch.

"Six, three, seven," Busby said.

I pressed a wad of gauze against his wound and it quickly turn from white to red.

"I need a shirt or something! There isn't enough gauze to stem the bleeding," I said. "Also, the flare gun is by my foot; I don't know how deadly it is, but I figure it's better than nothing."

Aldo was repeating the numbers Busby had said to himself while sliding the tumblers in place on the lockbox. It popped open and Aldo withdrew a sleek black Sig Sauer and one clip of 9mm ammunition. He plugged the clip into the bottom of the gun, pulling the slide back to chamber a round.

"Okay, yours is definitely better," I said.

Aldo did a side roll, squeezed off two rounds through the open door, then rolled again, landing on the other side of the door and quickly kicking it shut.

"He knows we're not such easy targets now," Aldo said. "He'll give it a good rethink before rushing us. There's not much cover between here and those trees."

"What about Saad?" I asked.

"If he keeps his head down, he'll be fine," Aldo said. "That shooter could've shot any of us, but he waited for Busby, so we know who his target is. He'll come for us. Saad is safer than we are right now."

Aldo was right. Assuming there was one shooter, Saad could slip out on the opposite side of the station and make a run for it with the building as cover. For us, there was only one exit, unless we tried the windows.

Busby was breathing fast, his eyes pinched shut. The smell of blood was everywhere. I started seeing the world through a red filter. I could feel Busby trembling. I was lost in it all.

"That's twice I've saved your life now," Aldo said. "The snake and this."

His words snapped me out of it. "If we get out of this, I'll buy you a coffee," I said.

"Not what I had in mind."

"Oh, that's right," I said. "I'll make it tea."

With both hands putting pressure on Busby's wound, I looked around for a piece of cloth I could put on it. There were sheets on the two bunks near Aldo.

"Aldo, toss me those sheets," I said. "And that pillow."

Holding the gun in his right hand, he threw the sheet and the pillow toward me with his left, never taking his eyes off the door. I slid the pillow under Busby's head and tore the sheet down the middle. More blood poured from out behind him than from the entry wound, making it clear that the bullet went straight through his shoulder. I put half the sheet on the entry wound, and the other half on the exit wound.

"That's a nice handgun for a primatologist," I said.

Busby's eyelids began to droop and he looked like he was fading out of consciousness. "I'm with the AFP," he said.

"Aldo, I need your help here, I have no experience with gunshot wounds!"

"Someone needs to cover the door," he replied. "Or you'll have more bullet wounds to worry about."

Given the reality of mass shootings in the U.S., there had been a greater push to incorporate treating gunshot wounds into standard first aid courses. There's a campaign called Stop the Bleed, created by trauma surgeons, to increase the awareness of proper techniques of gunshot treatment and to dispel certain myths. On the whole, the program was considered successful, but ultimately it was designed only to keep victims alive until first responders could arrive on scene. No help was coming for Busby and my knowledge was entirely theoretical. I could feel him slipping away.

Aldo moved like a chimpanzee across the floor, over the splinters of wood, shards of glass, and the long smear of Busby's blood. He crossed in front of the door and over to the window. In a low squat, he held the pistol close to his chest with both hands and peeked out through the shattered glass. He brought the gun up, resting the barrel on the sill as his eyes scoured the trees and bushes surrounding the research station. *Thwack*. Another shot rang out and a bullet lodged itself above the window.

The former royal marine ducked down and away from the window. The world around us fell silent. Aldo and I looked at each other. His brave face was better than mine, but he didn't have a dying man in his arms.

"We were here just to observe," Busby said. "We'd been getting reports of drug traffickers using Umboi as a holding station during rough weather. We wanted confirmation."

"I'd say you got it," Aldo said.

"Save your strength," I said.

He shook his head, at first wildly, then weakly. "I'm dead anyway," he said.

"No!" I told him.

"Laura, listen to him," Aldo said. "Go ahead, mate."

"Two days ago, a boat came in along the coast and used one of the rivers to sail deep into the jungle. PNG Defense Force had been watching the boat approach and were coordinating with my government. I thought it must have been loaded with cocaine, so I snuck aboard once I was sure the crew had taken shelter in the forest. But the hold was empty."

"So, they'd either offloaded their cargo already or took it with them?"

"The boat hadn't stopped since Hong Kong as far as we knew, so they hadn't offloaded their merchandise. They either took it into the forest with them or someone else beat me to the boat. The hold looked like it had been forced open ..."

The majority of deaths from gunshot wounds are a result of blood loss, not damage to any particular organ. It only takes between five and eight minutes for someone to bleed to death, and I was already behind. I packed the entry wound as best I could before trying to patch up the exit wound. Busby gritted his teeth, making a growling noise as I applied pressure. Some life came back into his eyes, and I intended to keep it there.

"You stay with me, Busby," I said to him. "Don't tap out on me yet, the fight's not over."

The bullet had hit him below the clavicle and above the heart. There was no way to tie off the flow of blood, like with a wounded limb. It made things harder, knowing that the wound itself was likely not a fatal one, but there was nothing we could do, in that research station on a remote island, to keep Busby from bleeding out.

He reached up, twisting his arm to put his hand on my shoulder. I looked at him, his face, his eyes, instead of the wound. Busby's lips moved but no sound came. The grip on my shoulder became weak until his hand slid off completely and made a mild thud against the floor beside me. His lips kept moving, even as his head tilted toward the two bunks.

"Stay with me, damn you!"

I looked at Aldo, who watched the door, ready for the shooter to come bursting through it, only glancing occasionally in our direction. Busby was dead, the result of nothing more than springing a leak. The part that gets you is the speed at which someone goes from being a person to being a corpse.

I stared at my hands, crimson with Busby's blood, the lines in my skin looking like ancient, dead rivers on Mars. The blood was beginning to coagulate and harden. My hands started to tremble, or maybe were trembling already, and I'd only just noticed.

"You did all that anyone could," Aldo said.

"You knew he was going to die, didn't you?" I whispered.

His mouth tightened and he gave a little nod. "I've seen it enough in the service," he said. "There was no way to stop the damn bleeding." He peeked up through the window and dropped down again.

"You didn't say anything," I said.

"What'd you want me to say? 'He's a dead man, forget him'? You filled his last moments with what we all want when we go, a beautiful woman bent over us, fighting to save us, making us think it was all worth it."

Chauvinism aside, Aldo was right. It wasn't as if I would have turned my back on Busby and let him die on the floor without trying. I'd spent the last few years of my life so safe, so comfortable, that I never found myself in a situation where I could fail so badly. When I took the job with NatureWorld, I knew it was a risk, I knew it might blow up in my face. I had no idea it could turn out with literal blood on my hands.

"There's still the three of us to worry about," Aldo said.

His words seemed to echo through my head as though my brain was nothing but a long, dark corridor with concrete walls. Where was Saad again? Were the others okay? Thoughts half formed were like static. I had lost all sense of place. "The three of us," Aldo said? Then it all came rushing back. "No, there's more than that," I said, looking up and over at him. "I have to radio Danny and the others and make sure they stay clear of here and bring the authorities."

"Wash the blood off your hands," he said, taking his canteen out of his rucksack and rolling it toward me. He then threw me a small rag, like a dishtowel.

"Get yourself cleaned up, then we'll radio the others."

I crawled toward the end of the station that faced the ocean and knelt. I poured the water over my shaking hands, then wiped them with the towel. I repeated the process again and again, the stain of blood never fully gone, just spreading to the towel, onto the floor.

I found some alcohol swabs in the first aid kit and tore a few open. As I tried to clean the residual, rust-coloured stains from my skin, the smell of the isopropyl alcohol competed with that of the blood. My skin felt dry, stiff like when the blood was coagulating, and for a split second I thought maybe I hadn't got the blood off at all. I scrubbed at my hands vigorously.

"You're good," Aldo said sternly, as though sensing that I was getting lost in the minutiae and losing sight of the big picture. "Let's get on that radio."

"Yes ... right," I said, throwing the swabs aside and reaching for the radio on the strap of my backpack.

It was gone. Unlike the missing satellite phones, I could clearly picture what happened to the radio. It was somewhere on the other side of the door, in the dirt, having fallen off when the shooting started.

"I dropped it," I said, "my radio. Let me have yours."

I stretched my hand out as Aldo reached around his beltline, pausing for a second before revealing that his hand was still empty. "Bollocks," he said.

"Is it possible that the gunfire could have been heard from the village?" I asked.

"Maybe, but I wouldn't gamble on it," he said. "The village is still a ways off, with lots of trees and hillside in between, not to mention the noise of the ocean to compete with. And that's assuming your mates are listening."

I surveyed the research station again. Could there be a trap door that I'd missed? No luck. There was only the one door, with the gunman and his assault rifle trained on it. The windows were an option. The glass had been mostly shot out on both sides of the station. Given that we didn't know the shooter's position, there was no way to know if he could see through the station if we tried climbing out either side.

"You could make it," Aldo said. "You climb out the window, be careful not to cut yourself, and hit the ground running. I'll lay down cover fire. If that shooter was half a marksman, he would have hit more than just one of us by now. If you move your arse, not in a straight line, mind you, you could get around the hill and run for the village while I shoot it out with the wild man of Borneo out there."

"You expect me to leave the two of you here?"

"You got a better plan?"

In my head, I pictured the area around the door of the research station, the steps, the ferns, other shrubs. There was a limited zone where either radio could be. Then I envisioned trying to get one, opening the door and signalling to the shooter my intention, then bounding left or right trying to snatch up a radio with bullets flying around me. If he was smart, the shooter would just keep the gun aimed at the door and pick me off as I scrambled to get back inside. There was, of course, one other option.

"Saad," I said, calling through the floor.

There was no answer.

"Saad," I said again, louder.

"Yes." His voice sounded far away.

"Can you see a radio on the ground near the door?"

I put my ear to the floor and listened for his voice. There was nothing, just the sound of the wind whistling faintly through the bullet holes in the shattered window.

"I see it," I heard after a minute or so.

"Can you reach it?"

"It's a few feet from the side of the station," he said.

"That's right in the line of fire," Aldo said.

"If we don't radio Danny and the others, they'll come looking for us," I said. "I can get it; you can cover me."

"I can get it," I heard Saad say.

"You won't be exposed?"

"I can do this," he said.

"Laura, when I get in position by the window, knock on the floor twice. That's your signal to make a grab at the radio, Saad. Do we all understand?"

I nodded.

"Yes," Saad said from beneath us.

Aldo got into the same half squat, the gun held close to his body and high so he could look down the barrel.

My heart raced. I was thoroughly powerless, risking Saad's life and leaving it to a stranger to protect him. I banged twice on the floor.

Gunfire broke out from the side of the hill. The bullets didn't hit the station, so they must have been chewing up the dirt outside. Aldo moved half a foot out in front of the window and fired three rounds into the jungle. He dropped down and we held still, just listening. My pulse, pounding in my ears, counted the milliseconds. I concentrated on controlling my breathing so I could hear every little sound, scratch, signal of movement.

"Got it!" Saad said.

"Are you hurt?" I asked.

"I'm fine," he said.

"You need to call Danny. Tell him to stay in the village with the others."

Saad's voice was audible through the floor. I could hear Danny's, as well, mostly him repeating "what?!" to everything Saad was saying.

Aldo was back by the window again, watching the hillside. "If the shooter hears that we're calling for help, he may try to come down here and finish us off before that help arrives."

"I'm assuming he doesn't understand what's being said."

"Even if he can't make out the words, we might be forcing his hand," Aldo said. "We should be ready."

We waited for what seemed like hours. The sun sank lower in the sky. Maybe the shooter was happy with hitting Busby. He knew Busby would bleed to death without medical attention. All he had to do was keep us pinned down. Once he learned we had a gun, finishing us off became harder, more high-risk. Or maybe he was waiting for the cover of night, since he'd have to expose himself in order to get closer.

"What's the AFP?" I asked Aldo, having guessed at the acronym already but wanting confirmation.

"Australian Federal Police," he whispered. "Like your FBI."

When a man bleeds to death, his life force pouring out and covering you, his occupation doesn't really matter. The question that did bounce around my skull was about Adam. Did he know Busby was undercover? He must have known that the range of Busby's knowledge was limited. Or had Busby passed himself off as a volunteer of some kind?

"He put something in his pocket," I said.

"What?" Aldo asked.

"He thought we weren't paying attention, but I saw him," I said. "Help me turn him over."

"Let the dead rest," he said.

"I'd rather see that he didn't die in vain."

"This is a thing with you, isn't it? You're the type that can't leave well enough alone, aren't you?"

"Aldo, you don't know the half of it," I said. "Now give me a hand."

Aldo and I gently turned Busby's body, as though it was somehow more respectful that way. I reached into his back pocket and found a smartphone. Whatever was on it was more important to Busby than bringing his pistol along. Was it just that its contents would expose him as an undercover cop? Or were there files, photos, emails or whatever that he needed to build a case and was unwilling to leave unguarded? It made sense in our digital age to a carry a backup of sensitive information.

The phone screen was badly cracked, probably a result of Busby falling after being shot. I turned on the screen, which seemed to function fine, the crack notwithstanding. The operating system was locked, not by password but by thumbprint scan.

"Goddamn it," I said.

"What?" Aldo asked, not looking at me but out through the shattered window.

"It's locked," I said.

"Password protected?"

"No, thumbprint."

"Oh," he said.

Busby's left hand, the side opposite from where he was shot, was the cleaner of the two, although there was still some blood on it. Taking an alcohol wipe from the first aid kit, I cleaned off the blood from his thumb and pressed it against the phone. The screen unlocked and I set Busby's hand down gently against the floorboard.

"Okay, we're in," I said.

The first thing I did was select the settings icon. I disabled the thumbprint-scanning function. The phone looked new, few apps and no files or downloads. It was like Busby bought the phone, walked out of the store, and came straight to Umboi Island. There had to be more to it, but sitting on the floor there in the research station, a murderer with an assault rifle looming outside, was not the right time to explore it. I put the phone in my pocket.

Aldo crawled across the floor, stopping short of the bunks, and reached out, tearing a sheet off the nearest mattress then pulling it across the floor. He bundled it up under his tattooed arm and crawled back over toward me. Setting the pistol down, he rose up slightly, spreading the sheet out and letting it fall on Busby's body. He tugged at the corners on his side, and I did the same for those on mine, until the body was sufficiently covered. Blood soaked through the sheet.

We both stared at the sheet and the body beneath it. The presence of it seemed to grow larger with each second, filling the silence between each breath. It reminded us that with every passing moment our chances of ending up lying on the floor beside Busby increased. Suddenly, everything outside the walls felt oppressive and dangerous. It was as though death was lurking outside, slowly crushing the research station and we would soon be crushed within it.

"Do we wait for nightfall or make a break for it now?" I asked.

"The lower the sun is in the sky the worse it is for us," Aldo said. "It's right in my face, so it will be harder for me to see him if he starts another firefight. If we wait too long, it'll be dark and he'll be able to get close without us seeing him."

"If we can't see him then he can't see us," I said.

"Were it just him and me, I might play cat and mouse," Aldo said. "But three people make a lot of noise. I reckon he's got himself a Kalashnikov. He's bound to luck out and hit one of us when we're blundering through unfamiliar ground. I'd rather make a break for it with the station between us and him and before the sun makes it too hard for me to get a bead on."

Aldo took the magazine out of the pistol and popped in one that was full. He put the other in his back pocket. He was preparing for a prolonged shootout, or at least for laying down lots of cover fire when we made a break for it.

Opening the tin box at my feet, I took out a flare, which resembled a shotgun shell, and loaded it into the flare gun. If Aldo and I were going to pull a Butch and Sundance, I wasn't going unarmed.

"I reckon our best bet is this," Aldo said. "You get ready to climb out that window. I'll pull open the door, giving the gunman a target. When I do, you go out and you and Saad run for it. I'll go back to the window and cover you from there. Run for the village, but stay apart, go over that hill in different places. Don't make yourselves easy targets."

"How good are you with that pistol?" I asked.

"If he reveals himself, I'll be as good as I need to be," he said. "I promise you that, even if it means I have to go out that door and take the fight to him."

"All this only works if he's alone and stayed within view of the door," I said.

"He'd be a fool not to keep the door covered. If he has backup on the way, then he'll sit on this place, watching the door from a spot where he can keep an eye on the trail, too."

"Okay," I said. "Okay, we can make this work."

Aldo nodded.

"Saad," I said into the floorboards.

"Yes?"

"Can you get over to the back side of the station? I'm coming out the window and we're making a run for the village."

He said something else, but I couldn't make out the words.

"What was that?"

"Nothing. Let's go," he said.

Taking my backpack off, I left it on the floor, sub-consciously picking a dry, bloodless patch. I needed to be able to move fast far more than I needed any of my gear. I kept Busby's phone and the flare gun. With my pack off, I faced the window, doing a plank on the floor for a moment to stretch out my legs. It was going to be the run of my life and I needed to be ready.

Aldo moved over to the door, leaning against the wall beside it, the pistol in his right hand with the bar-rel pointed at the ceiling. He closed his eyes for a split second, and his lips moved almost imperceptibly, as though he was saying a prayer. He reached out his left hand for the door handle.

As the door creaked open, I bolted. I didn't look back. Dropping to the dirt, I stayed still, looking beneath the research station as Saad slid out from under it. He'd ditched his backpack, too, but had the radio in his hand.

"You ready?" I asked.

He nodded.

We looked out at the trail that led toward the ocean. I gestured to myself, then to where I intended to veer away from the trail and crest the hill. Then pointed to him, and where I thought he should go over. He nodded again.

Was the shooter watching the now open door, or had he figured on us going out the window? I stuck close to the side of the research station, my hand in the air, and traced my route in my head. I took a deep breath, then whipped my hand down, a signal to Saad, and ran, literally, for my life.

The man hidden in the trees opened fire, his rifle booming as it spat bullets in my direction. Tunnel vision had set in and I could only see what was directly ahead of me. Aldo opened up on the shooter, his pistol sounding like firecrackers in comparison to the assault rifle.

I dove over the top of the hill and dropped onto my back, thick leaves and stems all around me snapping back into place. Saad came over a second behind me. He hit the ground and rolled. He got himself right again and looked around for me. I gave him the thumbs-up.

The gunfire continued, the booming of the assault rifle, the cracks of the bullets drilling into the wood walls of the research station, the sound of little pops in response.

"Go!" I hissed at Saad, pointing toward the village.

He hesitated, pulling back from me slowly as though we were attached, before turning and taking off down the hill toward the village.

I took the flare gun out of my pocket and crawled back up the hill. Peeking over the top, I saw a muzzle flare, like a horizontal campfire, from between two bushes. I pointed the barrel of the gun at it, then raised it so the flare would hopefully arc down onto my target. My chances of hitting him were one in a million. My chances of the flare starting a fire that would be even remotely useful as cover for Aldo were just as bad. But what are flares for? They're to get someone's attention.

I pulled the trigger and the gun spat out a ball of red-pink flame. It arced over the research station and fell to earth in the general direction of the muzzle flare. I ducked back behind the hill as the shooter fired back at me, a volley of three rounds, as if out of pity.

It seemed to be good enough. Aldo opened up on the shooter, three pops, then three more. There was no return fire. I reloaded the flare gun, then looked over the top of the hill again. Someone was moving through the trees, the branches and leaves swinging as they passed through them.

Aldo must have seen the movement, too. He fired a shot, then waited before firing again. I heard one more pop, then nothing. No noise, no signs of movement.

The shooter had used the foliage to conceal his escape in the direction of our camp.

Aldo dropped out of the window and ran toward me. I surveyed the surrounding hillside one more time before taking off back down the other side. It became a relay race as Aldo and I ran to catch up with Saad and meet the rest of the team in the village.

TWELVE

Intermittent expeditions on Umboi Island, Papua New Guinea, from 1994 to 2004, resulted in the compilation of eyewitness testimonies that substantiated a hypothesis that pterosaurs may not be extinct.

— Jonathan Whitcomb, "Pterosaur-like Creatures Reported in Papua New Guinea," Prweb.com, July 20, 2006

AS THE SUN SANK INTO THE OCEAN BEHIND us and whitecaps broke gently across smooth rocks and pale sand, the three of us ran toward the village, keeping our heads down. Aldo caught up and stayed beside us, but at a distance, glancing both ahead and behind, holding the pistol with both hands.

"Do you think you got him?" I asked.

"I doubt it," he replied. "He was either out of ammo or —"

"He hit what he wanted to hit and decided the rest of us weren't worth it."

The natural cover, trees, shrubs, bushes, and tall grass, receded the closer we came to the village. The three of us were suddenly exposed in a way I wouldn't have considered before Busby was shot.

Saad dropped back, making it easier for me to catch up. He then matched my pace and we ran shoulder-to-shoulder, Aldo covering us from behind. No matter what the challenge was, or how crazy things got, Saad was always there, steady, unwavering.

The ocean to the south looked strangely empty. At a time when fishing boats should be on their way back to the harbour after a hard day's work, the water was vacant. The boats were already moored, listing gently.

The peaks of the thatch roofs of the village grew closer and closer, like ships coming over the horizon. As the adrenalin began to ebb, it felt like the blood pumping through my legs had been replaced with concrete. Lactic acid built up in the muscles. We all began to slow, the sight of safety subconsciously cueing our fight or flight instincts to stand down.

Danny and the others stood against the wall of the largest building in the centre of the seemingly empty village. As we got closer, they began peeling away from the wall one by one. Aldo paused and scanned behind us, not just the trail but the hillside above the village.

My first priority was to get everyone together and make sure we were all safe. After a quick head count I noticed that we were one person short.

"Thank god you made it," Lindsay said.

Aldo herded us deeper into the village, as if to make sure we couldn't get picked off from a sniper on the outskirts.

"Mashallah," Saad said to himself.

"What are the odds that whoever shot at you will follow you here?" Danny asked Aldo.

"Slim to none, I'd say. Taking shots at a small group from an elevated position is one thing, taking on a whole village on level terrain is another."

"Let's just hope he doesn't know the village is empty," Danny said. "And where'd you get that gun?"

"We'll fill you in on all the details later," I said. "Where's Zach?"

"He knows the location of a ham radio apparently," Danny said. "It sounds like we need backup more than we thought."

"Any idea where the villagers went?" I asked.

"Some local boys wandered off last night and haven't returned," he said. "Whoever is fit enough to search and is not out on a fishing boat is looking for them."

"How many boys are missing?"

"Two," he said. "Your friends from yesterday."

"Michael and Joseph?" Saad asked incredulously.

"You make any other friends?" Danny replied.

"Try not to be a dick all your life, Danny," I said.

I heard the sound of a door closing and turned as

Zach exited a building nearby and jogged toward us. "Oh, thank heavens," he said, clapping a hand down on my shoulder. "You made it."

"Did you find a radio?" Aldo asked.

"I certainly did."

"And?"

"I notified the PNG Defense Force as to our situation. They're sending a boat as soon as possible, which, given their size, or lack of it, might take a several hours."

"They're coming here?" I asked. "To the village?"

"No, to the camp, since that's where the body is," he said. "Not to mention the foreign television crews. A country like this has to think about its reputation in the foreign media."

I realized then that the rest of the team didn't know about Busby. Saad had told them that we were being shot at, not that a man had died. In the moment, he'd only hoped to warn them off.

"There are two bodies now, Adam's and that of his colleague. The gunman shot him ... He didn't make it," I finished, trying to keep my voice steady.

"All right," Danny said, letting out a deep sigh. "Then I guess we should head back to camp before it gets dark."

"Is that such a good idea?" I asked. "There's a man with an assault rifle in the jungle somewhere between here and there." I turned to Zach. "And what about the missing boys?"

"Gilbert, one of the elders, is organizing another search party. There are men in boats going up and down the coast now, and several other search parties already looking where the boys have been known to play."

"They might be able to use some extra pairs of eyes," I said.

"Am I the only one not over the fact that there's a man out there trying to kill you?" Duncan asked.

In my first year of university, I took Introduction to Anthropology, taught by a young professor who was tall, lean, and handsome in a dorky sort of way. Although he wasn't a rugged mountain man type like my dad, or my mentor, Berton Sorel, he had his share of "war stories." The one that stuck with me was about the expedition he took to Madagascar to study lemurs. One night, he heard someone outside of his tent. He sat up just in time to avoid being hit by a shotgun blast fired from outside. He described the hole it left in the ground as being the size and depth of a Pringles can. It turned out that the man who fired the shot thought that Dr. Lehman was there to seize the land and prevent the gunman from earning his living hunting on it. Misunderstandings when scientists poke their noses around in other people's homes can lead to attempted murder. Could Busby's death be another example of that?

"We don't know anything right now," I said. "We don't know why we were shot at or who was shooting."

"I think it's safe to assume that Busby was shot because he's a bloody copper," Aldo said. "This must be about drugs if an Aussie's here undercover."

The team exchanged puzzled glances.

"Great, then we're not targets," Danny said.

"We can't assume that," I said. "Whoever wanted Busby out of the way might think he told us something he'd rather be kept secret."

"Both men from the research station are dead," Saad said. "Assuming they had any pertinent information, they've taken it to the grave. Would the shooter risk coming after the rest of us?"

"He'd be a fool to come here," Zach said. "The men of this village are skilled hunters. They're more than capable of handling one man with a gun. Then there's James Bond here." He nodded toward Aldo. "But you know, 'who dares wins.'"

"That's the bloody SAS," Aldo said.

"Let's clarify military mottos later," I said. "We should get the U.K. team and bring them here so we can wait together for the authorities."

"Gideon and the rest of the villagers aren't going to stop looking for those boys, so we can't count on strength in numbers," Zach said.

"Still, I think it's a safer bet for us all to be on one part of the island, rather than being vulnerable to being picked off one by one. Zach, you can always radio the authorities and tell them to come here first."

Zach nodded.

"Agreed," Aldo said. "I'm going to go back to camp to bring the others here. You lot stay here and help look for the missing boys."

"I'm coming with you," I said.

"I can move faster alone."

"I know you can, but you're not faster than a bullet. It's better to have two sets of eyes and two moving targets."

"You're crazy, girl," he said.

"Crazy is calling me 'girl,'" I said.

"All right, let's move out." Aldo turned quickly, without another word, and headed in the direction of the camp.

I didn't say anything or make eye contact with any of my colleagues. I fell in behind Aldo as though caught in the ex-soldier's wake.

"Better make that three moving targets," Saad said, jogging to catch up.

"You should stay here," I said.

"I can handle it," Saad said.

"No, you can't. Neither can I, for that matter, so why take another stupid risk," I replied. "You don't have to prove anything to me."

"I don't want you to think that I'm … fragile … after what happened in Lake Crescent."

"Are you nuts? If there's one thing you proved back there today, it's that you're a badass."

"It's just, you know I'm not much of an outdoorsman, and not a fighter by any stretch, but I can still be useful."

"Why do you think I drag you out here with me? I couldn't do this show without you. All of the risks I've taken since we've met, I've taken knowing that you wouldn't judge me, that you always had my back. Frankly, you're the only person I trust on this whole island."

"Then it's settled," he said.

"We better get a move on," I said.

Aldo jogged at a moderate pace. He knew from experience not to burn himself out, but instead to move steadily at a level he could maintain for a longer period of time over rough terrain. I had to push myself to keep pace. The jet lag, the injury from the night before, the fact that we'd been on our feet so much, it was all dragging me down. Aldo seemed to pick up on my thoughts, slowing slightly, allowing me to close the distance.

"Did you ever serve?" Aldo asked.

"No," I said.

"You handle yourself well, so I thought … You just don't seem like the average —"

"Woman?"

"I was going to say civilian. You're cool under pressure, good with navigation, survival, and first aid, and you can take a shock and still keep moving. Usually, that takes training."

"My dad was in the army," I said. "He didn't adapt well to home life, so much of my upbringing was a mix of basic training and boot camp."

"Your dad never taught you to handle a firearm?"

"I can handle long guns," I said. "We never covered pistols."

Aldo stopped in the middle of the path and turned to Saad and I.

"How about you, Saad?"

"I've never held a gun in my life," he said.

Aldo turned, keeping the muzzle of the pistol pointing down and into the bush. "Should something happen to me, I want you to take this." He seemed to be speaking directly to me. "See this little button near the grip?"

I nodded.

"Press it to eject the clip." He took the magazine out and showed it to us. There were holes in the black sides to show how many bullets were left. He popped the magazine back in the gun. "When you put in a new clip, you have to chamber a round by drawing back the slide." He pulled the top of the pistol back partway. "There's already one in the chamber now, so I don't want to clear it. But you get the idea." He raised the gun. "The rest is point and shoot. Use two hands and look down the sight. A good stance is key. Distribute your weight over both legs." Aldo mimed a correct shooting stance. Lesson over.

We didn't talk about what prompted that lesson. Telling off creepy Uber drivers or catcalling construction workers was reflex, a man in the jungle with a rifle trying to pick me off at a distance? It wasn't something I'd ever even thought about, let alone prepared for.

"I know this is not the sort of thing I'm supposed to ask," I said. "But, have you ever killed anyone, Aldo?"

"You're right, you're not supposed to ask that. Didn't your dad teach you that one?"

"He did. He told me to never ask a soldier that question. It was off limits, especially when I tried to talk to him about when he served."

"Your dad and I would get on fine," he said. "So why are you breaking this rule now?"

"There's ... there's this weight, this ball inside me. I feel it deep in my stomach and behind my eyes. I don't know whether I want to scream, or cry, or hit something."

He put his hand on my shoulder and looked me right in the eye. "I know. You want me to kill him." It was what I couldn't bring myself to say or even acknowledge.

"I want his blood spilled all over a floor, I want him to die alone on this island. I want him to pay."

Aldo let go and backed away. "That won't make the feeling go away. Booze won't fix it, either. Trust me."

He put his hand on his hip and stared at the dirt between his feet. "I thought I'd be a career army man. It wasn't the bloodshed on my last tour in Helmand that changed my mind, either. It was the blood I myself shed. You lose enough of your mates and you think you get the right to cast your humanity aside and become nothing more than a killer. To answer your question, I killed enough to stop seeing the people I killed as people. And you want to know the part that I struggle with? It's that I don't see any of their faces. I'm not haunted by them. I don't even see the faces of my mates torn apart by bullets or shrapnel. Whatever I lost over there I don't think I'm getting back."

"I'm sorry, I —"

"To be clear, if we come across the bastard that killed Busby, I will kill him without hesitation. You'd do well to remember that he'll do precisely the same to us given half the chance." With that, Aldo turned and walked away.

Saad and I hung back far enough to give the ex-soldier some space, but not so far that we could be easily picked off. The forest surrounding us was suddenly alive with hostile intentions. Every sound, every swaying branch seemed to signal danger.

It hadn't escaped me that the trails to the camp are finite. If the shooter was setting up an ambush, he'd have a fifty-fifty shot at picking the trail that we were taking. All he had to do was hunker down in the greenery with a good sightline and wait to pick us off. That's assuming that we were even targets. Maybe the shooter was content with killing Busby. Or maybe he circled back to the research station, looking for something inside.

The likelihood that he would go to either the camp or the village seemed low. What could he possibly want there? His objective must have been something in Busby's possession. The question became, then, did he think that whatever he was after was now in our possession?

Suddenly, a cry broke the silence, loud and close. The three of us dropped low, Aldo scanning the trees through the gunsights of Busby's pistol. Whatever it was, it wasn't human. But that didn't mean a human didn't startle the creature into making that sound.

After a moment, Aldo waved us on and we started back up the trail. He swept either side, scanning for any sign of danger. My eyes oscillated between his wide back and Saad behind me. My eyes were focused on Aldo at the wrong moment. When I looked back at Saad, the gunman was two feet from him.

"Whoa, whoa, whoa," he hissed, pressing the barrel of his AK-47 into Saad's back.

Saad put his hands up.

"You drop gun," he said to Aldo, staring intensely at him.

Without turning back to Aldo, I was afraid he was doing a soldier's math in his head. If he dropped his weapon, all three of us might be killed. A gunfight at that close a range would mean that Saad was dead for sure. Possibly me, too.

"Okay, mate, be calm," Aldo said.

"Now!" the gunman demanded.

The man was about my height, maybe a little shorter, with a helmet of thick black hair. His white T-shirt, stained with dirt and sweat, revealed lean, sinewy arms that gripped the rifle tightly. If he didn't have that gun, I was certain I could take him — not that I would have to with Aldo and Saad here.

"There," Aldo said.

Fear shot down my spine and into my stomach. With my back to him, I couldn't see what Aldo was doing, but if he was now unarmed, the chances of us getting executed in the middle of the jungle, a million miles from home, had increased drastically. If Aldo wasn't cooking something up, then it was down to me.

I was reminded of the first time my dad and I watched *Goldfinger*. There's a scene where James Bond is strapped to a table, a laser positioned above him, the beam slowly cutting through the table and making its way toward 007's junk. I was disappointed with his escape. I expected maybe a laser in his wristwatch or some other gadget to get him out of it. Maybe even some escape artist's trick. But all he did was talk himself out of it. My 007 education had started with the Roger Moore and Timothy Dalton films, so I was spoiled by exploding keychains and submarine cars, killer umbrellas and shark-inflating pellets. Sometimes, though, talk was all that was needed.

"What do you want?" I asked.

"Take me to the stuff!" he demanded.

He moved around Saad, in an arc, so that he could cover all of us at once. The gunman was smart enough not to get close enough for any one of us to grab hold of him. It wasn't like in the movies. I wasn't especially good at gun disarms anyway.

"We don't have your stuff, mate," Aldo said.

"I want my stuff!" he said.

A picture was forming, more like a jigsaw puzzle, but too many pieces were still missing. I guessed that the boat Busby mentioned was the one Michael and Jacob had seen. It seemed like too much of a coincidence that they were also missing at that very moment. How Adam's death fit into all this was beyond me, though.

"Why did you kill Busby?" I asked.

"He took the stuff."

"How do you know he did?" I asked.

"You shut up," he said, thrusting the barrel of the AK-47 in my direction.

"Let's make a deal," Aldo said. "I'll help you find your stuff and you let my friends go."

"How?" the gunman asked.

I could see Saad looking at me out of the corner of my eye. He was reading me, waiting for my cue to make a move. That gave me an iota of assurance that if I ever got around to having a plan, he was ready to roll with it.

"He gave us a cellphone just before he died. He said it was important. If he knows where your stuff is, the location is probably on that phone."

"Give it to me," the gunman said impatiently, as though suspecting that he was being tricked.

"It's not here," Aldo said. "We left it in the village. She knows where it is." He pointed to me. "Let them go and they'll bring it back here. Use me as a bargaining chip."

The gunman stood quietly, his brow furrowed, considering the offer. "I want the stuff!" he demanded again.

"We don't know about any stuff, but there's a chance that Busby did, and if he did, the location might be on that phone."

Gunshots echoed through the trees. The gunman cried out in pain and ran blindly into the forest. Aldo dropped to one knee, scooping up the pistol and firing at the swinging branches and crunching sticks. *Pop, pop, pop.*

Then nothing. No sounds, no movement. Only stillness in the forest.

"That was a close one," Zach said, as he emerged from the trees holding a Beretta. "Everyone all right?"

THIRTEEN

Over the years Biblical scholars have speculated about the nature of the creature in the Authorized Version as the "fiery flying serpent." The nexus of modern archaeological discoveries, ancient historical accounts, and recent cryptozoological research provides new insights into the identification and characteristics of this creature. Moreover, interviews and personal observations from a 2004 expedition that I led to Papua New Guinea convinced me that a fiery flying serpent still survives on a remote island there.

— David Woetzel, "The Fiery Flying
Serpent," January 2006

"YOU HIT HIM," I SAID. "HE WAS STILL MOVING pretty quick, though."

"Making it out of the jungle alive will be another thing," Zach said.

"It'll be a taste of his own medicine," I said.

Zach looked us over for wounds as we spoke. Aldo covered the trees. The gunman would be a fool to come back. His luck had run out.

"What are you doing here?" Aldo asked. "And where'd you get the gun?"

"Did you say thank you? Because I think I missed it," Zach said, his rivalry with Aldo made even more satisfying by the fact that he'd saved the ex-soldier's life.

"Thank you, Zach," I said, bowing. "Now can you please tell us what the hell is going on?"

"I don't really want to," Zach said.

Aldo took a step toward him, chin up and chest out — his macho stance. He kept the barrel of the pistol pointed into the dirt, so the posturing was an empty display of who thought he was the alpha.

Zach tucked his pistol into the waist of his shorts before concealing it with his T-shirt. "Drug smugglers," he said, sighing.

"I knew it!" Aldo said triumphantly.

"I know, mate, I know," Zach said. "Obviously I didn't want to broadcast it."

"Maybe things would have turned out better if you had," Aldo said, taking another step forward.

"You reckon? Well, hindsight is twenty/twenty, right? I'm the one who lost his partner, so how about you leave the second-guessing to me, all right. I can beat myself up, I don't need help."

"I'm sorry about Busby," I said. "We did everything we could."

"A gunshot out here is a death sentence. There's nothing you could have done," Zach said. "At least the bastard that got him will be rotting in the leaf litter sometime soon."

It made sense that Busby wouldn't be operating in such a remote place alone. I'm not sure what kind of special access Australian police required to operate on Umboi Island, but it seemed to extend to at least two cops. If we were lucky, maybe there were more, or maybe some PNG cops in place here, too.

"Do you have any backup coming?" I asked.

"Busby was the only other officer on the island. I radioed in from the village. The PNG authorities know everything I do. They're sending some of their own drug enforcement team. With what happened to Busby, my own superiors will also be flying in. Unfortunately, they won't get here quick enough for my liking."

"It was lucky you showed up when you did," Saad said.

"It wasn't luck," Aldo said. "He was using us as bait."

"Is that true?" I asked.

"Think of it as me watching your back," Zach said.

"Fucking hell," Aldo said. He turned around, placing his hands on his hips and looking up into the branches that reached across the top of the trail.

I was too grateful to be alive at the moment to be pissed at Zach, but I was sure it would come later. The recklessness of it seemed right out of an eighties buddy cop movie.

"Danny and the others are still in the village?" I asked.

"They'll be bunking there for the night," Zach said. "With any luck they'll find the missing boys and the whole village can turn in early."

I looked up, where a purple dusk had replaced the brilliant blue sky. Night came on like a shift change in these remote places. The diurnal creatures punching out as the nocturnal ones punched in. We were bleeding what little light was left. "It's getting dark fast," I said. "We need to move. If the man wasn't going toward the camp before, he might be going there now to get help."

Aldo and Zach looked at each other, then started to jog up the trail. Saad and I followed. With each step I began to realize that we could have just gone back to the village to meet up with the others. We could have done more good there than we could in the camp. But we just kept following the two men.

"Hold up," Zach said as we approached the camp.

"You don't know I'm a cop," Zach said. "Clear?"

Aldo nodded. Zach looked back at the two of us.

"I blew my cover because I had to stop you all from getting killed. No reason to make it public knowledge. We need to tell them everything else, but please just leave out that one detail."

Satisfied with our nods, Zach continued on, both he and Aldo moving faster now. My legs didn't have much left in them as we approached the plateau. It wasn't just fatigue, but the after-effects of shock on top of all the running and hiking. Sweat glistened on Saad's face and he was breathing heavily as we arrived at camp.

Aldo and Zach split up to secure the opposite sides of the camp.

Brodie came out of the commissary, a look of shock on his face when he saw the gun in Aldo's hand. "My god," the photographer said. "What on earth is going on here?"

The Scotsman's loud voice drew a crowd, with doctors Agahze and McTavish emerging from the cataloguing tent. Soon everyone else had joined us. Zach jogged back from the other side of the camp, giving Aldo the all-clear. Celine followed behind him.

"Let's get everyone into the commissary," Aldo called out.

Everyone moved en masse toward the large central tent.

Once inside, Aldo and Zach stood together near the door, whispering. It seemed they decided that Zach would stay outside and keep watch.

As Zach left and took up his post, Aldo turned to me. "Tell them, Laura," he said.

All heads turned toward me. I felt like I was leading a tent revival. Unfortunately, it was all fire and brimstone, with no promises of salvation.

"By now, you've all heard about Adam Tarver," I said. "You have also probably heard that we lost the ability to communicate with the mainland, so my team and I went into the village to use their shortwave radio to report Tarver's death."

The researchers stared on, curiously, without any disruptions and little fidgeting. It was a group that was used to lectures, to waiting until the end before asking questions. It was that end that I was afraid of.

"We have called in help," I said. "But we ran into two snags …"

Aldo made a face, not appreciating my soft sell of the situation. Dr. Agahze tilted his head, imploring me to elaborate.

"Two of the boys from the nearby village are missing," I said. "Members of my team have joined in the search. I hope they can be found before nightfall."

"Why the gun?" Brodie called out. "You don't go running around with one of those things cos some lads have run off."

"Where did you even get that?" McTavish asked.

"So, that's the second snag," I said.

"You're really bad at this," Aldo muttered.

Saad shot him an angry look.

"It's my first time," I whispered back.

"The three of us," I said, gesturing to Saad and Aldo, "went to the research station where Tarver had worked to inform his partner about his death. Someone starting shooting at us and Tarver's partner was killed."

Everyone's facade of calm curiosity disappeared in an instant. Based on previous experience, it was about the time that fear would cause someone to find a way to blame me.

"I don't understand," McTavish said before turning to Aldo. "What the hell is she talking about?"

"Let the lady finish," Aldo said.

"We learned that unlike Tarver, his partner wasn't a primatologist, but an undercover police officer. He only told us after we relayed the information of Tarver's death, and he himself was mortally wounded. That's his firearm Aldo's holding."

"And what happened to the shooter?" Brodie asked.

"We were forced to shoot him," I said, not giving the specifics to maintain Zach's cover.

"Is he dead?" Celine asked, leaving no room for ambiguity.

"He escaped into the forest," I said. "But he's wounded. I don't see how he could survive the night without medical care."

The U.K. team looked frantically at one another, then over their shoulders toward the exit.

"I don't think we'll see him around here again," Aldo added.

Whether it was because Aldo was better known to them, a former soldier, or just that he was a man, his words seemed to settle the crowd.

"How long until help arrives?" Dr. McTavish asked, raising his chin a little and looking down his nose and through his glasses at me.

The audience was, for lack of a better term, captive. Stillness in a crowd, by its nature, was short-lived. The motion afterward would be commensurate with how much they liked my answer. I knew how much that would be even before I said it.

"Members of the PNG Defense Force should be here by sun-up," I said.

The stillness shattered, my words like a brick thrown through a bus shelter.

"Sun-up?!" Dr. Agahze said with genuine shock.

"By Jove!" McTavish added. "There's a murderer on the loose!"

I pictured the gunman, wounded, lying in the fetal position on the forest floor somewhere with only venomous snakes for company.

"We also have to keep in mind that we aren't their first priority. First there is a dead member of the Australian Federal Police. Then there are the missing boys …"

Suddenly, it felt like I'd woken up in the middle of a chess match. Pieces were being moved around the board, part of an elaborate stratagem, and we were just reacting. Chess was Saad's game, not mine.

"What are we going to do until then?" McTavish asked Aldo.

"We carry on," Aldo said. "It's just a few hours. We'll move some of the light standards out of the lab and the commissary. We'll have to run the generators longer than normal, but we have some extra petrol. I'll take the first watch. The likelihood we're in any more trouble is slim, but proper preparation prevents poor performance."

The 5 Ps was a favourite saying of my dad's and seemed to be a transatlantic hit, too, at least among military men.

"So, we're supposed to act like nothing's happened?" Brodie said.

"Not exactly," I said. "Stay in groups, watch each other's backs. I understand much of your shooting is nocturnal, but it's best not to leave the camp until help arrives."

"We can't call off the helicopter," McTavish said. "It'll be flying in from the mainland before sunrise, re-fueling at the Bunsil Airstrip, where we're scheduled to meet it. We set out at dawn."

"With the missing boys, we may not be able to count on help from the locals, but if you can heft your own kit, I don't see why you can't meet the chopper," Aldo said.

I pictured Bunsil on the map, at the southeast of the island. McTavish and his team would have to set out in three hours or so if they hoped to lug their gear through the rainforest and rendezvous with the heli-copter at dawn. It would be tough even with villagers to guide them, but without them or Zach and Aldo, the task would be a daunting one.

"I'll help with the gear," Dr. Agahze said.

"Me, too," Brodie added.

Before we knew it, the bulk of the U.K. team had decided that they'd pitch in. Whether it was the idea of safety in numbers or the fact that there was a dead body in one of the tents, it seemed that the thought of being away from the camp was better than holing up inside it.

"Well, that looks settled," I said to Aldo and Saad.

"Aldo," Dr. McTavish said. "We can't just leave the camp unguarded, even for only a few hours."

"I'll hold the fort, so to speak," he said.

McTavish rejoined the others and soon became the centre of attention. Aldo, Saad, and I went outside with Chris and Joshua in tow and joined Zach, who stood at the corner of the tent, at the intersection of two trails.

"That went well," Zach said.

"We avoided out-and-out panic," I said. "I'll take that."

"It'll be two hours to the airstrip, at least," Zach said. "By the time I get back, backup should be on the island and probably here in the camp."

Aldo, Saad, and I shared expressions of surprise.

"You're going with them?" I asked.

"Your job entitles you to pick up and leave, not mine. I might have to play the guide a little longer."

"The man who killed your partner is still out there," Aldo said.

"Which is exactly why I don't want a gaggle of microscope jockeys traipsing through the jungle alone. I'd rather see as many of them to safety as possible." He put his hand on Aldo's shoulder. "I trust you to keep the rest safe. I know you held him off at the research station. I stopped by on my way back here, I saw the shell casings."

Zach then turned to me. "And I saw that you did everything possible to keep Busby alive. I will be sure to get word to his wife and boy and let them know." He smiled weakly. "But I'm stuck on this island until I get reassigned, and this thing is far from over." With that, he went inside the tent to confer with Dr. McTavish and the others.

"You've done all you can for now," Aldo said to me. "You and Saad should get off your feet. I'll be along shortly with a game plan."

Neither Saad nor I put up a fight. We walked back to the tent where the men slept. Danny and Duncan wouldn't be using their cots, so that freed one up for me and for one of the women on the U.K. team. I doubted any of them would be tucking into bed anytime soon, not after the news we'd just delivered.

The tent was empty when we entered. Saad asked to see Busby's phone and I handed it over, happy to be rid of it. The owner of it had died in my arms and it seemed as though he died for nothing. Saad adjusted his glasses and held the phone high, as though he might take my picture with it. "Unless there's some kind of hidden folder, I don't see any reason he would want to take this with him," he said. "And if there is a hidden folder, it's probably heavily encrypted." He tapped the screen, swiping in various directions. "This looks like my mom's phone," he said. "The background is practically empty, only default apps. But unlike my mom's phone, there aren't a million outgoing calls in the call log."

I stared at the back of the phone, the phone's case rather, which was black like the phone itself. "Look under the case," I said.

Saad dug his thumbnail under the corner and peeled it away from the phone. He then offered it to me. In the bottom corner was a loose memory card, too large for the phone, but perfect for a digital camera.

"I'm an idiot," I said. "I don't know why it took me so long to think of that."

"You were shot at and a man died right in front of you," Saad said.

"You're right, I'm not having a very good day."

"Let's go get a camera and see what's on this," he said.

We knew we'd find one of Chris's cameras among his gear. He seemed to have one extra tote for bric-a-brac on every expedition, aside from his video camera and whatever special equipment we were using. I suppose a good cameraman never knows exactly what he'll need, so had better come prepared.

Saad dug through the tote and removed a small digital SLR camera and handed it over to me. "Here," he said.

I slid the tab at the bottom of the camera open, removing the memory card that was inside and replacing it with the one Busby had concealed in his phone case. Giving the device a once-over, I turned it on and accessed the photos stored on the memory card. I scrolled through image after image of crab-eating macaques, some at play, others eating, some fighting or mating, it was difficult to tell which.

"Why try to hide these?" Saad asked, looking over my shoulder.

We were thirty images deep, but there were 158 to sort through. By the seventieth image the macaques had disappeared and now it was just jungle, trails, a river running from all the way up the volcano that might have once channeled lava. There were shots of the coast, of small bays and inlets, one with a small fishing boat moored in the distance.

"That's the river where the boys shot the Ropen video, isn't it?" I asked.

"It sure looks like it," Saad said.

Then we came back to more pictures of the interior of the island, trails with dense foliage on either side, almost cavernous. The pictures didn't seem to have been taken for the natural beauty contained within each, but as though Busby was scouting locations.

"What's that?" Saad asked, pointing at a dark circle obscured by a branch in the foreground.

"It looks like a cave," I said.

We scrolled through several other images of the mouth of the cave, but there seemed to be no pictures of its interior. Busby never ventured close enough to get any better shots. We scrolled through more and the ridges and vegetation began to look familiar.

"Isn't that where we were positioned the last night? Near the camera traps?"

"Yes," I said.

Each new picture brought us closer to the camp, but none were taken from inside it.

"Why was Busby so interested in our camp?" I asked.

I took a closer look at the date in the top left corner of the screen.

"Or should I say in the U.K. team's camp, we weren't even on the island when these pictures were taken."

Once we passed the hundredth photo mark, we started to see familiar faces. There were pictures of Aldo, Zach, Celine, and Brodie. In each shot, the U.K. team members and their guide were alone, in various parts of the island, all seemingly unaware that they were being watched.

"How often have you been out of the camp by yourself since we got here, Saad?"

The screen on the back of the camera was reflected as a small, glowing square in his glasses.

"Not once," he said.

"Me, neither."

"I've seen Brodie go off on his own, to film."

"And he has a camera with him in every one of these pictures," I said. "Still, I can't help but think back to what Dr. McTavish let slip, about Brodie's gambling problem. You've gotta wonder what kind of debts he might have racked up."

"It's certainly possible," Saad said.

"But what about the others?"

"You think they were persons of interest in Busby's investigation?"

"They were on Busby's radar for some reason," I said. "If he was a cop, as he claimed, then he must have had reason to spend his time photographing these people." I continued scrolling through the photos. "Hello!"

"Is that —?"

I stopped on a photo of a boat with forest in the background. The shot hadn't been taken along the coast, so likely on a river or in a cove.

"If Adam was murdered, maybe it was because someone thought he was also undercover."

"That's definitely possible," I said.

A voice came from outside the tent. "Laura?"

It was Aldo.

Powering off the camera, I slipped the memory card out and put it in my pocket.

"You'd better get some sleep," he said. "I'll be back for you in three hours when it's your turn to take watch."

I managed to get about two hours of sleep, each cot and tent being just about the same as another. Saad was still sound asleep when Aldo came in. His linebacker build was recognizable even in near darkness, backlit by the glow of the light standards we'd stationed around the camp for extra security. Aldo paused on his way toward me, as if deciding how to wake me for my turn to keep watch. I sat up and saved him the trouble.

"Are you taking Saad with you?" he asked in a whisper.

"Let him sleep," I said, standing up.

I expected Aldo to protest, but he handed me Busby's pistol and took my place in the cot.

"Suit yourself," he said. "There's one round in the chamber and a full clip."

Taking a flashlight I'd found in Danny's bag, I moved quietly toward the flap. I think Aldo was sound asleep before I even left the tent.

My heart sped up as I stepped out into the night. Every sound outside seemed like a potential threat. Artificial light messes with a person's night vision. It gives an unnatural hue to things. The effect on the edge of the forest played tricks with my eyes. I moved up behind each standard, like I was taking out sentries, only to be cloaked within the light they cast. The idea was always to be where I could get a good look at any intruder but he couldn't get a good look at me.

Every tent flap was closed, even those where work was still being done, light bleeding through the gaps. The generators hummed. The light gave the camp the appearance of a baseball park during a night game.

The emptiness of it all gave my mind room to move and expand. It wasn't easy to stay focused on the task at hand. I started thinking about those photos on Busby's camera. Why had he taken so much trouble to photograph Brodie, Aldo, and Celine, and even his own partner, Zach? And what of that abandoned boat? Zach might be easy to explain away, it could just be a matter of documenting where they'd been. Perhaps he knew he was being photographed and just went about his business. I wanted to ask Aldo if he'd been aware he was having his picture taken, then it dawned on me. If he's a person of interest, the less I told him, the better. Sure, he'd saved my life, but he might not have done it out of the goodness of his heart.

Suddenly, there was a sound, like fabric on fabric. I turned around, raising the gun and the flashlight, crossing my arms at the wrists. But there was no one there. I approached the corner of the commissary, taking a wide step around it. Two palms were pointed in my direction, the face tilted back and down, shying away from the beam of my flashlight.

"Celine," I said. "You could have got yourself shot."

"I was surprised to see you take the watch by yourself."

"You thought I might like the company?"

"I thought you could use it."

"I can manage just fine," I said.

"Well, I had difficulty sleeping …" She stood in the dark, looking down, like a submissive puppy. "I think we got off on the wrong foot," she said. "I know I can come off as brusque."

"Brusque?"

"It means —"

"I know what it means. I'm not sure you do. Your behaviour has been far beyond brusque."

She brought her left hand up to her cheek, maybe to wipe away a tear I couldn't see. "This has been … trying for me, to say the least."

"You lost someone," I said.

"I can't pretend that Adam and I were anything serious, just a flirtation in a faraway land."

"Still …"

"Still, it wasn't supposed to end like this."

Celine stepped away from the tent and took a step past me, like she wanted to go for a walk. I moved to let her by, but wasn't convinced that I should join her in a stroll. She stopped and looked at me again, realizing I wasn't about to go with her. "He wasn't the monster Lindsay probably told you he was," she said.

"You'll forgive me if I don't take your word for it," I said. "I'm not saying that I'm glad he's dead, but don't expect me to suddenly feel too much sympathy. If he did kill himself, that tells me that he knew what he did was wrong and couldn't live with it."

Celine's little-girl-lost vibe disappeared and was suddenly replaced by the cold hardness of someone keeping their rage on a leash. "That's not it at all," Celine said. "Adam felt terrible about what happened with Lindsay. It was a misunderstanding. He was young and in love, she didn't —"

"Don't call that love," I said. "I'll settle for unhealthy fixation or obsession, but don't try to make this the unrequited love of a teen movie."

"And what do you mean 'if'?" she asked.

"What?"

"I just realized, you said 'if he did kill himself.' You think he might not have killed himself?"

"It doesn't add up for me," I said.

We had "shared" enough. I tried to walk around her to carry on with my patrol, but she grabbed my arm, her elbow tight against her body. It was a tell, a give-away. Not just reflex. She knew how to handle another person, how to use her strength to its fullest. It was like she was daring me to yank myself free. But sometimes words beat force.

"That's my flashlight hand," I said. "There's a gun in the other one. You might not want to grab me. I've had an awful last twenty-four hours."

She released her grip. "I'm sorry, I just … I would really like to know why you think he didn't kill himself. I'd prefer to think he was murdered, to be honest. That sounds morbid, I know, but I'd hate to think his last moments were spent drowning in self-loathing and hopelessness."

The submissive-puppy face was back. It should have been clear that suicide was far too much of a coincidence. Two men in a research station on Umboi Island both end up dead within twelve hours of each other, with all means of calling for help either missing or sabotaged. The signs that Adam had been dragged and even drugged didn't really matter. The question was, why stage the fake suicide for one, then shoot the other. Would it not have been easier to kill them both either in their sleep or as they observed the macaques?

"Get some sleep, Celine," I said. "You have a big day tomorrow."

She looked at me in a way, I don't know, so penetrating that I couldn't be sure she wasn't reading my mind. I have tells, too, and perhaps she was picking up on them. But she didn't linger long before turning back toward the tents, leaving me alone to patrol the early morning hours.

FOURTEEN

For years, reports of living pterosaurs have come out of Papua New Guinea and its surrounding islands. Of particular interest is a creature said to live on Umboi Island which is just off the mainland coast. Locals have reported sightings of a creature they call *Duwas* or *Ropen*. With a wingspan said to be up to 29 feet, the dark-gray flyer possesses two leathery, bat-like wings and a long tail with a diamond-shape on the end. Also noted is a head crest and dermal bump, a tooth-filled beak, and razor-sharp claws.

— T.S. Mart and Mel Cabre, "The Truth Is Out There: On the Wild and Divisive World of Cryptozoology"

ALDO BEAT THE SUNRISE AND SAAD WASN'T far behind him. The three of us watched the awakening dawn from the centre of the camp, each of us with an eye on one of the three trails leading in and out. The U.K. team began to stir, heading first to the commissary, then congregating at the southernmost edge of the camp, near the trail that led down to the beach.

"Looks like they can't get out of here quick enough," Aldo said.

"Dead bodies have that effect on people," I said.

"What a luxury it is to be able to walk away from a body," Aldo said. "It's something else when it's your mate and his family is counting on you to bring him home, no matter what state his body's in."

"Thankfully neither of us will have to deal with this. I don't know that I could. The authorities should be here shortly. I should think Adam's body will be gone before McTavish and his party get back."

Saad and I borrowed backpacks that the U.K. team were leaving behind, filled canteens with water, and went to the mess tent for snacks we could take with us. I also took one of Chris's cameras so we could compare the photos to the landmarks we recognized. Aldo watched us from the centre of camp, the pistol tucked into the waistband of his khakis.

The call of a hornbill echoed eerily in the distance.

"We'll be back as soon as possible," I said as I approached Aldo.

He looked at me and nodded. "I'd come with, but someone needs to stay here."

"Understood," I said. "After about an hour, we should be in radio range of Danny and the others. They might even have rendezvoused with the police already and be on their way here."

"Speaking of police, did you give Zach Busby's phone?"

Saad and I looked at each other. "Shit," I said.

Aldo put his hands on his hips, giving me a disappointed look with a matching sigh.

"Zach will be coming back, won't he?" Saad asked.

"I'll radio him while he's still in range," Aldo said. "We should at least let him know that we have it."

"Sounds good," I said.

Aldo extended a hand toward me. "Better leave it here, don't you think?"

There was a chance I was handing a crucial piece of evidence over to a killer. Then again, there was a chance I was being paranoid. After all, I had been through a trauma. I could be forgiven for being slightly irrational after finding a body and being shot at. I handed the phone to Aldo.

"Be careful with it," I said.

He smirked.

It was either the morning sun or Aldo's gaze burning the back of my neck as we started out of camp on the trail leading to the village. The tree cover soon became thick enough that we were sheltered from the sun's rays, but the humidity of the jungle was stifling.

"That's too bad," Saad said. "We can't use the photos to —"

"Don't sweat the small stuff," I said. "The phone is just a phone."

"But the memory card …"

"Is safe and sound," I said, winking at him.

As the trail took us toward the ocean, I recognized the last stretch of trees where the forest had been thick enough to conceal the gunman, allowing him to get the drop on us. I looked for signs of that confrontation, shell casings from Zach's Beretta maybe. There were dark stains splattered across the leaf litter. At first I thought it was where Zach had shot the gunman, but that didn't track. He disappeared so quickly into the brush that he didn't have the opportunity to leave so long a trail.

"Do you see that?" I asked Saad. "It looks like the gunman doubled back after we left."

Saad stepped over and looked at the droplets, following them as they led us toward the village.

"We spent all night afraid he'd come for us, but instead he backtracked. I wonder if he knows this part of the island any better than we do. He took a big risk to use the trail, where he'd have no cover. I'd expect someone who knew the terrain better to stick to the trees."

"It could be his wounds were too severe, he didn't have time to be careful," Saad said.

The blood trail became easier to follow as the forest thinned out and more light filtered through the canopy. The longer it went, the more certain we were it was the gunman. A wounded animal wouldn't keep to the trail for so long, and anybody else would have been crazy not to come into our camp with such an injury. All the locals knew where to find us.

"Laura, look." Saad pointed into the foliage on his side of the trail. He crouched down and looked beneath a medium-sized plant with teardrop-shaped leaves so green and thick it looked artificial. On the underside of the leaves were husks of what were once ants. A tiny tendril grew out of each, like an antenna. I recognized at once that they'd been stricken by a fungal infection, one I had read drove them like mindless zombies to the highest point of the plant. It was fascinating in a way that made my skin crawl, but I soon realized that wasn't what Saad was calling my attention to. In the leaf litter on the forest floor lay an AK-47 assault rifle.

Saad took a step back and I moved closer. He looked apprehensive, like the gun was a venomous snake that might strike out at any moment. As I bent down, I saw there was dried blood on the stock, the handle, and the barrel.

"Laura, maybe you shouldn't —"

I picked up the rifle and took the magazine out. It was still loaded. I checked the chamber. There was one round in the pipe. An AK-47 sure beat the flare gun I'd been carrying around in my pocket.

"He didn't ditch it because it was empty," I said.

"Maybe he was trying to blend in," Saad said. "If he needed first aid, he could pretend to be the victim of a shooting, rather than the shooter."

"That's possible," I said. "But look at it. What's missing?"

Saad shrugged.

"There's no strap. He'd have to carry it the whole time. If he was trying to keep pressure on his wound, he'd have to abandon the gun or risk bleeding to death."

"So at least we know he's unarmed," Saad said.

I stuck the magazine back in the rifle. "He still might be dangerous."

My dad first took me grouse hunting in Grant County, northeast of Yakima, when I was eight years old. He didn't let me handle a rifle at so young an age, but the experience normalized gun-handling for me. It wasn't long after that I started shooting grouse, pheasants, and rabbits, graduating to deer before the distasteful aspects of hunting outweighed my desire to make Dad happy. By then my love of cryptozoology had begun to match his, and I didn't need to try so hard. Still, the hunting and tracking skills he imparted in me often come in handy in ways I'd have never predicted.

The trail of blood droplets soon meandered off the trail and into the forest. I motioned for Saad to stop, my index finger on the trigger guard of the gun. The AK-47 weighed about eight pounds, but it was a heavy eight pounds — the weight of the power to take human life.

I went first, trying to keep at least ten feet between Saad and I. Whatever last-ditch effort or trap the wounded and cornered man might try was sure to be sloppy, wild, ballistic. The blood droplets were clear against the leaves and moss, with some rolling down the side of a rust-coloured termite mound. There was a spot where the leaf litter had been cleared and mud was clearly visible. I saw where the imprint of a boot had intersected a trail of deep, three-toed tracks, something like a cassowary maybe.

About twenty feet ahead I noticed the entrance to what looked like a small cave, one of the thousands of pores in the limestone that served as the foundation of Umboi Island. The blood droplets led toward the cave mouth, but seemed to disappear just before the entrance. The gunman must have grown weak from the blood loss, seeking cover where he could rest.

I crouched down, pointing the barrel of the gun ahead. The entrance looked swept out, its occupant pushing out the husks of nuts that it once fed upon. It was light enough to see ten feet in. There was no body, no blood.

"Laura, here," Saad whispered. He had come up behind me and circled to my right. He pointed to the ground, to a trail of blood that ran between his legs.

"He's either hiding in the jungle or he's delirious," I said.

We followed the droplets again as they led us in a familiar direction. I should have realized where he'd go. Yes, he would seek shelter, but not being from the island, he was likely to pick the one place he knew would be empty, at least for a short time, a place where he was likely to find what he needed to patch himself up.

"He's trying to get to the research station."

It might have been faster to backtrack to the trail then run toward the station. For our sore muscles and lack of a good night's rest, we were still in better condition than our quarry. But it was just as likely he was lying near death against one of these trees.

We moved cautiously over the unfamiliar terrain. The wounded gunman was just one of several things that could kill us out there. The drops of blood continued parallel to the trail. We'd be in the clearing where the research station sat in fifteen or twenty minutes.

"What are we going to do?" Saad asked.

"Find the man who killed Busby," I said. "And find out what he knows, about the missing kids, about this whole mess."

"But, beyond that," Saad said, "are we going to, like, arrest him? You're not going to …"

He let his words disperse into the humid air.

"We'll tie him down if we have to," I said. "Then we'll patch him up. I'd love to see him pay for what he's done."

The trees thinned out at the crest of a hill. Below was the clearing where the research station stood, looking the same as when we'd left it. It occurred to me then that we were roughly where the gunman had been when he took those shots at us. I moved down the hill slowly. Brass shell casings glinted in the sunlight. One of those shells had carried the bullet that killed Busby.

More blood drops led up the stairs of the research station, the door drifting open in the breeze coming through the trees from the water. Was it the gunman's blood or Busby's? I waved Saad behind me and to the right. Staying in the dirt, I came up beside the stairs and looked through the gap in the door. Nothing.

Going around the other side of the steps, I could see another swath of the research station floor. Busby's body where we had left it, lying under the bloodstained sheet. From that side, I could push the door open farther, and did so with the barrel of the AK-47. The entire station was visible now, except the two bunks.

Climbing the three steps, I raised the rifle high. Whatever I knew about clearing a room with a rifle I learned from TV. Martial arts had taught me to do whatever was necessary to get close to an assailant holding a gun in order to execute a disarm, so as the assailant, I knew the reverse was true. Peering through the door, I made sure my right side was clear. I moved inside quickly, pivoting out from the open door in case someone was concealed behind it. The gunman was on the left bunk, his wound covered in a bandage that had soaked through. His heavily tattooed arm kept pressure on, his hand now covered in blood. His eyes passed over me but barely seemed to register my presence.

"Saad, in here!" I called out.

Saad was up the stairs in two bounds, his hands clenched into fists and held high.

The gunman was rambling in a language I didn't understand. I had English and high-school Spanish and French under my belt. Saad had English, Urdu, and a few words of Punjabi from his mother and a little

Arabic from his Quran studies as a child. But what I heard sounded almost like a Chinese dialect.

"That's Mandarin," Saad said. "I can make out the words for 'uncle' and 'sorry.'"

I looked at him with what must have been curiosity on my face.

"My niece, Miraal, is learning Mandarin."

"Well," I said, "we could use her right now. See if you can get Danny on the radio, find out where Lindsay is. She definitely knows Mandarin. Maybe we can get her to translate from there."

Saad unclipped the radio from the strap of his backpack and tried Danny. I moved toward the wounded man in the bunk.

"Hey, hey," I said.

The man's eyes rolled slowly toward me.

"How many more of you are here?"

One bloody finger raised from the hand clutching the wound.

"Saad?"

"Danny's trying to locate Lindsay. They've split up. They're still looking for the missing boys."

I turned back to the man on the bunk. Busby said the hold of the boat was empty and it looked like someone had taken what was inside. If the gunman and his partner suspected that it was a local who robbed them, then maybe they'd taken the kids, hoping to trade them for the drugs. What better way to enlist the co-operation of the people who knew the jungle like the backs of their hands.

"Where are the kids?"

"No kids," he said faintly.

"The boys, the two boys, where are they?"

He pinched his eyes shut and shook his head.

"Saad, tell Danny to send help here, now," I said.

"What do you want?" I asked the man.

"We want stuff back," he said. "Cocaine. In bags."

His words seemed to confirm what Busby had said. Someone had taken the drugs out of the hold when the smugglers came ashore. It seems they suspected Adam and Busby, since they both wound up dead. But why stage Adam's death to look like a suicide? Whoever did that had to know about Adam's history with Lindsay. And where did the kids come into it? It didn't make sense.

"Saad, how's that help coming?" I asked.

He turned to me and shrugged. "There's nobody close by," he said. "They're all searching for the missing children."

"Where's the backup Zach radioed for?"

"No help has come, they said. It's still just them and the villagers."

I crossed the floor, stepping carefully around Busby, and held the rifle out toward Saad. He looked at me like I was handing him a snake. He hesitated before clipping the radio to the strap of his pack. He took the gun from me, careful not to put his fingers anywhere near the trigger. I gathered up what I could from the first aid kit on the floor and went back to the wounded man, pressing gauze against his wound.

"Water," I said, handing him my canteen.

When Busby died, I wanted nothing more than for the man who shot him to get what was coming to him. Now that he had, all that rage seemed to flow out of me as the blood flowed out of him. We're all just scared little mammals, trying to carve out a life for ourselves and to hold on to what little we've got. The drug smuggler was going to die. There was no help coming, and he'd already lost so much blood. He was going to die in the same spot where he had killed, completing a circle that I felt but didn't understand. And just like with Busby, I was there to make sure he wasn't going to die alone, without that last shred of human dignity. Joshua was wrong. We don't need faith to have compassion, to believe in an inherent dignity and a connection between each and every member of our species.

The man suddenly grabbed my wrist. He gave it his all, I could tell, but his grip was as weak as a toddler's. The intensity in his eyes did all the heavy lifting.

"Please, sun," he said, "the sun."

I've heard the expression "a dying man's last request" in so many books and movies, but it's not the sort of thing you expect to be made of you. I could have broken his grip easily and left him there to die. There's no question that had he hit me with one of the rounds he fired into the research station the day before, he'd have left me to die. No last requests. But I read in a comic book once that no one deserves mercy, that's what makes it mercy. I also have a personal rule, which is to only be a deliberate asshole once a day. It wasn't even noon, so I didn't want to waste my one shot just yet.

I started lifting him out of the bunk.

"What are you doing?" Saad asked.

"He wants to die with the sun on his face," I said.

Saad reached a hand out to help.

"Keep back," I said. "Keep me covered. If he tries something, or his buddy arrives, be ready." Dad taught me a lot, but paranoia might be at the top of the list.

Saad went over to the doorway, leaning out only a little, not leaving himself exposed. He ducked back inside and gave me a wide berth. "Clear," he said.

I was turning him into a regular commando.

The gunman and I took the stairs slowly, but his legs gave out by the second step and we both ended up in a cloud of dirt.

Saad rushed over to the door and I swear he was ready to ventilate our prisoner. There was a look in his eyes like a coyote's when you get too close to its den.

"I'm good," I said. "I'm good."

The gunman either didn't care to get back to his feet or didn't have the strength. He crawled on his hands and knees toward the middle of the clearing, where the rays of the morning sun reached down and touched the earth. He picked his spot, then turned over onto his back and looked up at the sky. He was dead within a minute.

"Saad, can you bring a sheet out?" I asked.

He disappeared from the doorway as he moved deeper into the research station. I was happy to have his eyes off of me while I rummaged through the dead man's pockets. He had no wallet, no knife, nothing needed to survive. That told me that he had his valuables stashed somewhere close by. He wasn't carrying anything he couldn't afford to lose. There was a balled-up piece of paper in his pocket. When I opened it, I immediately recognized the logo at the top of the sheet. It was the same as the one on the flag that snapped in the wind behind me, that of the IWSF. The paper had a list of names on it, the date from last Tuesday written across the top. The names were first names and nicknames. Was it some kind of code?

"Don't move," a familiar voice said from behind me, the accent American.

I put my hands up, letting the scrap of paper drift to the ground. Saad appeared in the doorway, holding the rifle with the sheet bundled under his left arm.

"Come out here and put the gun down nice and slow."

Kneeling down, Saad put the AK-47 in the dirt by my feet. The sheet fell down to the ground. Saad rose up again with his hands up, his eyes looking toward mine for some idea what to do.

"Turn around," the voice said.

"Hello, Zach," I said before turning.

"I do a dandy American, don't I?" he said, his accent back to normal.

"Very convincing," I said. "You should be in Hollywood. What leading man in American movies isn't British or Australian these days?"

"The Ryans," Saad said from behind me.

"What?" I asked.

"The Ryans, Gosling and Reynolds. They're Canadian."

"This is a nice chat," Zach said. "Now give over whatever you took from that cop."

I feigned confusion.

"I'm not pissing about here," Zach said.

I reached into my pocket and found the memory card. "Honestly, it's not that incriminating," I said, holding it up.

"Let me be the judge," he said, reaching out with his free hand.

I dropped the card into his palm. He closed his hand and drew back quickly. He then half pushed, half punched Saad, who stumbled toward me. Still brandishing the pistol, Zach backed up the trail. With a distance of about twelve or thirteen feet between us, he put the memory card against the grip of his pistol and snapped it in two. The pieces fell into his left hand. He tossed them off the ridge.

"Now, suppose you tell me what gave me away," Zach said. "Why didn't you hand over the SD card with Busby's phone?"

"I didn't really suspect you, to be honest," I said. "I thought Aldo might have been involved in this somehow and that there was some kind of double-cross happening. Sure, I suspected that you were lying about being a cop, but I had no proof. What confirmed it for me was the fact that help hasn't arrived. You never radioed for backup, did you? In fact, I wouldn't be surprised if the radio in the village was sabotaged."

"Their boats have radios, so it won't be too hard for them to call for help," he said. "I just needed a little time, that's all."

It seemed like our little talk was coming to an end. Zach was eying the trail and the surrounding hillside like he was about to act. I hoped he just wanted to run, but I wasn't going to take the chance that he might shoot us to protect his secret. I had to remind him that the secret was already out.

"But now there's a whole village full of people that know you lied about calling for help, so everyone will be suspicious of you."

"I was tired of this place anyhow," he said. "Where I'm going now, nobody will recognize me, and nobody from these parts will be able to find me."

He bent his wrist and tilted the Beretta back toward himself, examining the barrel that protruded slightly. After glancing down at the weapon, he pointed it back toward me. There was no closing the distance before he could get a shot off.

"Now, what to do with you two?"

"Three people have died because of these drugs already," I said.

"Couldn't be helped," Zach said. "As weird as it is to say, I only feel bad for the cop. He was just doing his job. That tosser Adam was a scoundrel, easily convinced by my associate to disable Busby's radio and steal the satellite phone. He thought he'd run off into the sunset with Celine in one hand and a few million dollars in the other. And the smuggler killed one cop and probably a few more along the way, so no one will shed a tear for him."

Celine? Of course she figured into it. The question remained, was she in the driver's seat or just along for the ride? If I was lucky, Zach would go on talking.

"So, it's all worth it?"

Zach smiled, bringing the gun toward his forehead and wiping the sweat from his brow with his forearm.

"I made a mistake many years ago and I've been paying ever since. I thought this island was better than prison, but it's just a lusher, greener prison, and who knows how long that will last as the logging companies come in."

"Just like Greenpatch Hill," Saad said.

"That's right, mate, just like Greenpatch Hill. Just like people to muck up paradise. Nothing beautiful lasts, so I'm going to at least get what I want out of this whole thing."

"That's oddly philosophical," I said.

"I'm a complicated fella," he said.

He kept the gun levelled at me while stepping back to put more distance between us. "I'm also a nice guy, so I'll give you three seconds to run," he said. "One!"

We wasted the first second out of sheer surprise. I heard the hammer of the pistol draw back and click into place as I grabbed Saad by the arm. We ran for the corner of the research station. My breathing and heartbeat were so loud that when he called out "two" it sounded as though it was a voice over a phone left dangling, like in a movie.

"Three!" he said, firing a round into the wall of the station.

The second round kicked up a plume of dirt. We stopped by the corner stilt that held the station up off the ground. It was a single log, not wide enough to provide much cover. I knelt down and reached for the flare gun, looking for Zach's legs and praying he wasn't aiming for ours.

But he was gone. I dropped to all fours and crawled underneath the station, flare gun in hand. There was nowhere to run if he was looking to pick us off. My best bet was to take him out. Even if I failed, it would give Saad a chance to get away.

"Laura!" Saad called in a harsh whisper, too late to stop me.

I looked out at where Zach had been standing, but he was gone. Only the body of the last guy who tried to kill me at that very spot was left. The AK-47 was gone, too. The lowest branch of the Terminalia near the northbound trail swung unnaturally hard in the gentle breeze. It looked like he'd done the math and decided a few wasted bullets were better than two more bodies. If he was to be believed, he'd only killed one person so far — a drug smuggler who would have easily killed him if their positions had been reversed. I'd like to think he spared us for reasons other than his own self-preservation. Although, shooting American TV personalities would bring down more heat than he was likely prepared for.

There was no other movement. Even still, part of me wondered if Zach might pop out from behind a tree and finish us off. I emerged slowly and stood with my back against the side of the research station. Saad came around the corner and joined me.

Lying on the ground between the dead drug smuggler and I was the scrap of paper I'd taken from his pocket. It rolled gently across the ground. I scooped it up before turning to Saad.

"Should we follow him?" he asked.

That was way too close and I wasn't about to risk Saad's life again, or my own. "No, let's get back to the others. We're not the cops. Right now, we're more useful as witnesses."

We started off toward the village, moving quickly down the incline.

"It's too bad we lost the memory card," he said.

"Yeah, I guess I'll have to buy the network a new one."

"Wait. That was the network's memory card?"

I stopped and bent down, then reached into my sock and took out the card that Busby had been careful to conceal. "Sooner or later, someone would want to trade for whatever evidence Busby had collected. It seemed like a good idea to carry a decoy."

Saad looked down at the SD card in the palm of my hand, a smile on his face. But his smile faded quickly and he looked up at me quizzically. "What do we do now?"

"We need to rendezvous with the rest of the team and get in touch with the police."

"Who knows how long it'll take the cops to arrive."

"I guess we have to hope that someone in the village got word to the Coast Guard or the police," I said. "Zach played us all brilliantly."

"Like a chess game."

"Exactly," I said.

FIFTEEN

My initial first priority on Umboi Island was videotaping and photographing a ropen. After one week, realizing the creature was too elusive, I started videotaping eyewitnesses instead.

— Jonathan Whitcomb, "Another Perspective on the Fiery Flying Serpent," *Creation Research Society Quarterly* 2, no. 42 (September 2006)

THE VILLAGE STILL RESEMBLED A GHOST town. Over a dozen boats listed in the harbour or rested on the shore as the fishermen took part in the search for the two missing boys. We'd radioed ahead, and as expected, found only Danny, sitting on the steps of the main building.

"I'm relieved I didn't have to send a search party out for you two next," he said, pointing at me with the antenna of his radio.

"Still no luck finding Michael and Joseph?"

Danny shook his head. "Duncan and Lindsay joined the search. That Cousin Tobias guy is interpreting for them."

"And you're just sitting here?" I asked.

He waved the radio at me. "I'm coordinating."

"They've been missing for a day now," I said. "I doubt they just wandered off."

"Do you think they were taken?" Saad asked me.

"With everything else that has gone on, to think this is just a coincidence is —"

"Stupid?"

"I was going to say *wishful thinking*, Danny."

"I hate to say it," he said, "but a thousand things can happen to kids wandering around a place like this. Why would someone want to kidnap them?"

"Two reasons come to mind," I said.

Opening up my backpack, I took out the camera and popped the SD card into it. Saad leaned in and looked at the screen as I shuffled through Busby's photos. Some of the places in the pictures were familiar to us, some were not. We now knew to focus on the photos with Zach in them.

"We have to assume all these photos were taken relatively close to camp, the research station, the village, and the river where the drug smugglers took their boat during the storm," I said. "Both Zach and Busby were never too far from those locations, so the caves in the photos must be nearby."

"Those aren't the caves we passed on the trail, are they?" Saad asked.

"They don't look like them," I said.

"The search parties have already covered that trail," Danny said.

"What about farther east along that same trail?"

"Zach told us that the bridge was out," Saad said.

"Sure, that's what he told us, but what if he knew another way around? Nobody would search there, because why would the boys go there if there was no bridge. But that fact would make any cave near there the perfect hiding spot."

"Hold on, so you think our guide took those kids?" Danny asked.

"It's either that, or a second smuggler has them and wants to trade them for the drugs Zach stole. Either way, we need to find out where Zach hid the drugs."

"That's crazy," Danny said.

"It's worth checking out," Saad said.

"Let's head out," I said to Saad, "if we stay here too long, I don't think I'll be able to get moving again."

"That sounds like a good reason to stay," Danny said. "Laura, you've run yourself ragged and almost been killed how many times now? You might want to rethink this martyr complex you have going on."

"I'll ponder that long and hard on the flight back," I said. "For now, those boys are still out there."

Danny reached into his pocket and took out a granola bar. "We're on channel six," he said, throwing the bar at me. "Call in if you find anything."

I snagged the bar out of the air. "Thanks. Let the others know where we're going."

He was soon out of our sight as we crossed the village and started up the trail that led up to the crater of the volcano. Saad began falling behind on the steep incline. It felt like we hadn't had a minute's rest. By the time we reached the trail Zach had showed us the night before, I had very little energy left. Saad, covered in sweat, was on the verge of collapse.

"Let's take a breather," I said, searching for tracks in the damp soil.

After a short rest, we started off again, now following a pair of fresh tracks that led toward the east end of the island. Soon the trail split, with one branch leading down to the river. Beyond it we could see the bridge Zach had spoken of, or at least what remained of it. Logs bound together with rope had, up until recently it seemed, spanned the river, anchored to tree trunks on either side. One log still attached moved with the flow of the current like a fish hooked on a line. It was only a matter of time before the rope snapped and the current carried the remaining log over the edge of the waterfall just downriver.

"How do we get across?" Saad asked.

The water was still high from the storm two days earlier, but it was not flowing as swiftly as it had been the day before. I looked at the rope that remained and wondered how we might be able to use it to cross. But, unless Zach had gear stashed nearby, he hadn't used the rope to cross the river, otherwise it would still be anchored in place.

The fresh tracks we'd been following seemed to end abruptly at the edge of the trail above the waterfall, as though whoever made the tracks jumped off the edge to the river below.

"What are you doing?" Saad asked as I started to climb down onto the rocks just off the trail.

"I'm playing a hunch, as my dad used to say."

Saad hurried over, kneeling on the cliff's edge and watching as I climbed down.

There was a light dusting of soil covering the limestone and I noticed impressions in the dirt where someone else's shoes and clothes had brushed it away. I saw a split in the bedrock, a horizontal crack that ran from my position to behind the waterfall. It was the perfect size to slip a foot into. I secured a handhold and began to inch across the ledge.

The limestone, smoothed by years of running water and wet from its spray, was slippery. I continued slowly, following the ledge around the bend and into the waterfall itself. The water was surprisingly cold considering the climate. It woke me up and motivated me to go faster.

There was a half-pipe carved into the limestone behind the waterfall, not a cave proper, but wide enough that I could walk easily to the other side. It was damp, a sheen of water over everything, impossible to tell whether anyone else had passed through recently. I turned back to call for Saad, only to see him breach the wall of water and join me.

"Danny's right," he said. "You are crazy."

"Maybe, but you followed me, so what does that make you?"

He shrugged, smiling widely.

"We should be quiet from here on in. Who knows how far Zach's cave might be from here."

We climbed out the other side, staying silent and keeping low. The trail here was clear, but turned sharply up ahead. There was no telling what was around the bend. I waited for Saad to catch up, my back against the limestone, the flare gun in my hand.

I took the corner quickly, my left hand out as a signal to Saad to stay put. It was all clear so I waved him along. There was a series of caves carved into the limestone on this side of the river, three gaping doorways in close proximity to one another. But only one had wet footprints leading into it. I pointed the tracks out to Saad and put my index finger to my lips. There was no talking him out of following me, so I didn't try. And I didn't want to.

We moved slowly and deliberately, following the tracks that led inside the bowels of the dormant volcano until they blended in so much with the smooth, damp rock of the cave floor as to become indiscernible. As we got deeper in, the cave grew wider. Darkness closed in around us. I kept my left hand against the wall and peered ahead, trying to make out shapes. I heard a sound like fabric being dragged against rock.

I froze. In the dim light, I saw Zach. He was standing with his back to us. He'd set a flashlight on the floor, and I followed its beam to a stack of duffel bags. Beyond Zach I saw two pairs of legs pointing in opposite directions against the limestone floor. They were skinny, dark with white socks and white shoes. The drug smugglers hadn't taken the kids, Zach had! *The devil you know is always preferable*, I thought. I looked back at Zach and saw that the pistol was tucked into his waistband. The AK-47 was nowhere in sight.

I stuck close to the cave wall, making sure not to block Saad's line of sight. He needed to see everything I could and there was no communicating with him. I waited for Saad to get closer before handing him the flare gun. Taking him by the arm, I guided him against the cave wall, taking his wrist and raising the flare gun toward Zach.

With him covering me, I moved slowly forward toward Zach, hoping to snatch the pistol from him and take control of the situation before anybody got hurt. As though sensing my presence, Zach suddenly spun around, his hand shooting for the gun handle tucked against his lower back.

Kicking doesn't make much sense in a real confrontation, except if it's a kick to the nuts. Unless you're a Saturday-night tough guy challenging people to step outside because they looked at you funny, most confrontations are already at close range when they begin so kicks are less useful than elbows, knees, and open-hand blows. However, when you have to close a distance fast to prevent a man from drawing a gun, kicks can come in handy.

In Muay Thai it's called a teep, a front kick that can be used like a jab to find range or stop an opponent from getting closer. Or it can be a push kick. I chose to kick Zach square in the pelvic bowl, folding his body while sending it back. He fell straight down on his ass and it was enough to foul his draw. As he scrambled for the gun, I knew better than to reach down and try to wrestle him for it. Instead, I moved toward his prone ankle, stomping down on it with all my weight like I was trying to start an old V-twin motorbike.

Zach cried out in pain as I felt a crunch under my boot. He stopped trying to get the gun and instead cradled his leg. It was as my instructor always said: "A disarm is any technique that makes your opponent unable or unwilling to use his weapon." A gun wasn't doing Zach any good with his ankle broken; even if he did shoot us all, he wasn't going anywhere fast.

The gun had fallen onto the cave floor between the boys and I. Michael, who was facing me, stared wide-eyed at me, crying out under his gag. Before Zach could think about the gun again, I kicked it toward the cave entrance.

"I'll have you and your brother out of here in a second, Michael," I said.

I heard a sound from outside the cave and wheeled around to see the gun, which was lying at the outer edge of the circle of light cast by Zach's floodlamp, being lifted by a pair of phantom hands. I watched as the barrel was raised and swivelled until it was pointing right at Zach.

"I thought you might need a translator again."

Lindsay stepped into the circle of light.

"How did you find us?" I asked, letting out the breath I'd been holding.

"Danny told us the general direction you'd gone," she said, "and I didn't need to be an expert tracker to follow all the foot traffic that led to this cave."

Lindsay gestured at Zach with the gun. "Did you kill Adam?"

He groaned and reached down at his injured ankle.

"Hey! I asked you a question! Did you kill Adam?"

"No," he said. "That was Celine's job. She slipped him a little cocktail to make him easier to manage. She staged the suicide. My job was just to make sure none of you saw it."

Of course it was Celine. She was always a little extra, a little too sweet on Adam, a little antagonistic toward us. Even a little too caring when we spoke earlier that morning.

"But you stole the sat phones," I said.

"That was a team effort. We needed a communications blackout to get you out of camp."

"You killed Adam as a diversion?" Lindsay asked, incredulous.

"Two birds, one stone. We killed him because he wasn't one of us," he said, pointing to the scar on his neck. "He knew too much. He wanted too much and he was no longer useful. His death served two purposes."

"And you took these boys to make sure the villagers would be too busy to help us," I said.

"We knew the drug traffickers who survived the storm would come after us. We didn't know where they were, but we knew they were using that drone to try to find us. So, we wanted to fill the jungle with people, searching all the hiding places in the area."

"You could have got someone killed," I said.

"The smugglers were more likely to run than fight it out."

"Tell that to Busby," I said.

"He had a fifty-fifty chance, didn't he?" Zach said. "He might have got the better of them."

"How did they know to even look for Busby?" Saad asked.

I took the bunched-up paper that I'd found on the smuggler out of my pocket and held it out. "When they took the drugs out of the hold, they left this behind, as a clue. Just as taking the boys was a ploy to misdirect the villagers and Adam's death was made to look like a suicide to misdirect us. You were right, Saad, it's been a big chess game the whole time, and we were all just pawns."

In that moment, it felt really good to have broken Zach's ankle.

"Whose idea was it to put Adam on my cot?" Lindsay asked, a tremor in her voice.

I watched her as she shifted her weight side to side and let out a sob. Her hands were trembling as she held the gun. I was afraid she'd squeeze a round off just from nerves.

"Answer me!" she said, turning the gun and firing a shot deep into the dark heart of the cave.

Both boys screamed.

"Christ!" Zach cried as the shot echoed. He turned and looked at me.

"You better tell her," I said. "I couldn't possibly get that gun away from her before she shoots you, and I'm not catching a bullet to save your skin."

"You crazy bitches!" he said, then looked at Saad.

Saad took two steps back and folded his arms as though his union-mandated fifteen minutes just started.

"Clock's ticking," I said.

"That was Celine's idea. She really knows how to get in someone's head, you know, plant the seeds of chaos."

"She should shoot you for that 'seeds of chaos' line alone," I growled.

He looked from me to Lindsay.

"Drill him one in the knee," I said.

Lindsay moved her aim from his head, down his body, until the barrel's trajectory stopped right above his knee.

"Shit, I'm not serious, Linds! Don't shoot him!"

She let the gun hover there for a second longer.

"I know that," she said, smiling.

It was a far scarier smile than I thought her capable of.

"What does Celine have to do with this?" I asked.

Zach looked at me, pain and anger written all over his face. I took a step toward him and raised my foot near his injured ankle. He shot his hands up at me pleadingly. "Okay, okay! I don't know what good it can do you anyway, you'll never see her again. We were partners. She got close to Adam and recruited him to our cause. Of course, he didn't realize it."

"Her split would be more than an entomologist would see in a lifetime," Lindsay said.

Zach looked over at her and started to laugh. She pointed the gun at his knee again and he shut up immediately. He was holding something back. I knew it.

I gestured to Lindsay and she handed me the gun.

"Go untie the boys," I told her.

Lindsay helped the boys to stand, removed their gags and bindings, and led them out of the cave. I stayed to cover Zach as Saad went outside to radio for help. I waited until it was just Zach and I before I ordered him to his feet.

"You broke my bloody ankle!" he said.

"Use the cave wall for support," I said.

"I'm regretting letting you live."

"I haven't made up my mind about your fate yet," I said.

Zach rolled over onto his hands and crawled over to the side of the cave, dragging his left leg across the ground. I picked up the nearest duffel bag and slung it over my shoulder. I stayed a safe distance from Zach, should he try a desperate attempt to get the gun away from me. But he seemed to know he was beat. He made his way toward daylight, using the cave wall for support and placing each foot carefully. I fought the urge to tell him to pick up the pace. It wouldn't have made a difference; we were at least ten minutes away from the others at this point.

Zach made it to the mouth of the cave and stuck close to the wall. I gestured with the barrel of the gun and told him to sit down. Soon I heard what sounded like half the village coming up the trail from the opposite direction that Saad and I had taken. The boys' father and mother were near the front of the parade, passing Cousin Tobias, who led the way, and running to their children with open arms and tear-filled eyes. It felt like a win. Cousin Tobias smiled as he watched the reunion, walking straight toward us.

He looked at Zach, who was sitting against the cave entrance looking defeated, then walked over and unzipped the duffel bag I'd left on the trail.

"There are more inside," I said.

He turned to the villagers and said something in Tok Pisin. A half-dozen men filed into the cave. It didn't take them long to start coming out with duffel bags in their arms, piling them against the opposite side of the cave to where Zach sat, cradling his ankle.

"My, my," Cousin Tobias said. "Marvellous work." He clapped three times.

"Can I have that gun?" he asked.

"I've grown attached to it," I said, "or at least attached to not having other people shooting at me with it."

"I guess I should explain," he said. "My name is Tobias Uhu. I'm a sergeant with the provincial police. I was Busby's partner in this joint operation."

Busby had said there was someone else on the island with him, and since we could now rule Zach out, it made sense that a local cop would be his contact. I nodded at Lindsay and she handed the Beretta over. Cousin Tobias ejected the magazine and cleared the chamber before tucking the gun into his pocket. He obviously believed Zach was injured enough that he could be handled without a gun, and with children and so many civilians around, it was probably wiser not to use it.

"We'll take this man and the drugs back to the village," he said.

I looked at Lindsay, who nodded, then I handed the flare gun over.

"There's still another smuggler out there," I said.

"We have his boat," Cousin Tobias said. "It's secure in the harbour near the village. My guess is he'll head north to find a boat off the island and never come back. After losing millions of dollars' worth of drugs, he has bigger worries."

I watched Lindsay as she stood between the cave mouth and the waterfall, her back against the limestone and her arms crossed. Anyone else, under other circumstances, would be awestruck with the view from where she stood — the waterfall, the trees, the ocean beyond. But Lindsay was in a little hell of her own, one not of her making, and as she stared off, it seemed to me as if she was looking for a way out.

"I'm sorry —" I started to say.

"Maybe you were trying to protect me or whatever, but try clueing me in next time, instead of leaving me out," she said.

"Understood."

SIXTEEN

The very "best" Ropen accounts related so far involve substantial prompting and leading of witnesses and a great deal of confusion over what is being claimed. In fact, some published interviews between investigator and eyewitness read like textbook examples of how not to do an interview.

— Darren Naish, *Hunting Monsters: Cryptozoology and the Reality Behind the Myths*, Serius, 2017

WITH THE BOYS FOUND AND THE BOAT SECURED, along with eleven duffel bags filled with cocaine, it seemed like a job well done. The men from the village had dragged the bags out of the cave and lined them up along the trail like body bags after a natural disaster.

"That's about forty-five million dollars' worth of co-caine right there, I reckon," Cousin Tobias said, after unzipping each bag and looking at the bricks of co-caine double-sealed in plastic.

"What's this?" he said, unzipping the last bag.

Instead of bricks of cocaine, he removed a trail cam-era and a survey net. Lindsay walked over and looked inside the bag.

"This isn't our equipment," she said, "it must belong to the U.K. team."

"So essentially one bag is missing," I said, "assuming the traffickers didn't bring a spare bag that Zach hap-pened to use to store the stolen equipment."

"Only one bag," Cousin Tobias said, "but with a street value of almost five million dollars."

"Zach alluded to a mistake he made years ago that he'd been paying for ever since. What if he needed the money to pay off some sort of debt?" I said.

"Busby told me that Zach was involved in some sort of gang. He was busted, then became a witness for the Crown in exchange for leniency. He was forced to leave Australia and hide out here, under a new identity given to him by the Australian government."

"So, he hoped to steal from one gang to ingratiate himself with another," I said.

"That's a dangerous game," Cousin Tobias said. "But it was too much of a temptation for him not to try. The big challenge would be getting the drugs off the island. Whatever his plan to move the drugs was, it seems that he could only move one bag at a time, hiding the rest in the cave, meaning the missing bag, if there indeed is one, is already in transit."

"That's where the U.K. team comes in," I said. "He told us Celine Yi, the team's entomologist, had been his accomplice," I said. "It's a safe bet that she has the missing drugs."

"And she's in a helicopter, flying to New Britain with the rest of her team as we speak," Lindsay said.

"Now she'll get all the glory," I said.

"Not if we get to her first. She must have a boat waiting for her on New Britain," Cousin Tobias said.

"You don't think she'd hijack the helicopter?"

"Too dangerous," Cousin Tobias said. "Too easy to track. And the helicopter wouldn't be carrying enough fuel to take her far enough. A boat is more likely to go unnoticed and get her out of the country safely."

Cousin Tobias took out a sat phone from his back pocket. I almost couldn't believe it worked, but I heard the tones as he pushed each button. Apparently, there was still one functioning phone on the island. We knew the authorities would be hours away. As Tobias filled in his superiors about New Britain, I wondered how much more time it might take them to get there and if they had the resources to send boats to both islands. The remote nature of the islands and the sparse police presence was the reason drug traffickers used them in the first place.

• ● •

The village was bustling, as all the search parties had returned. Word had spread about the boys being found and everyone was out on the street waiting to greet them.

Danny sat in the middle of all this activity, the one person without a smile, his usual indifference plastered on his face. But compared to Zach, who'd limped back with a villager on either side of him, Danny was downright jovial. "I sent the cavalry," he said, waving his radio again. "I see you won the day, Laura? The kids are safe, the villain captured, the drugs confiscated."

"It's not over yet," I said.

"Excuse me?"

"Celine swapped out the U.K. team's equipment for bricks of cocaine and is using their helicopter to get the drugs off Umboi Island."

"Why is it always the beautiful ones?" he said, shaking his head.

"Jesus, Danny," Lindsay said.

"Sorry, it must be the heat," he said, looking up at the sky.

"What's this about Celine?" Aldo said, appearing behind me. I noticed his shirt had a collar of sweat stains, his hair was wet as though he'd just showered, and his skin was red from his forehead all the way down to his neck. He must have run all the way here.

"She's taken five million dollars' worth of cocaine is what. She's using the helicopter to get the drugs off the island."

"Say again?" He crossed his arms and furrowed his brow.

Before I could say anything, Cousin Tobias appeared, Zach in tow, his escorts still flanking him. The three men took the prisoner inside one of the buildings, then Cousin Tobias came back out and walked over to us.

"What the hell is going on?" Aldo asked.

"Two of your comrades stole fifty million dollars' worth of cocaine from some very nasty people," Cousin Tobias said.

"Zach?! And Celine?!"

"I'm afraid so," I said. "But only Celine is getting away, and only with five million dollars' worth of drugs, if that makes you feel any better."

"What about the others?"

"I'm fairly certain it was just the two of them," I said. "Oh, and Adam," I added.

"No, I mean the others on the helicopter." He looked from me to Cousin Tobias. "We have to reach them and make sure they're okay."

"What's the plan?" Cousin Tobias asked.

"Is that boat in working order?" I asked, pointing toward the harbour.

Cousin Tobias nodded.

"How far between where they're going and the shore?" I asked Aldo.

"It's not the distance, it's the elevation," he said. "The chopper is taking the team to a plateau half a click up from sea level. From there the plan was to follow a network of trails up the Langila volcano and into one of the valleys that is essentially cut off from the rest of the island."

"I doubt Celine will stick to that plan," I said. "She'll probably break away from the team at the first opportunity, taking the drugs and working her way down to the coast."

"She'll want to get to the nearest harbour," Cousin Tobias said. "That'll be the one at Sag Sag."

"Can we get there in time to stop her?" I asked.

"Doesn't matter," Aldo said. "This is a rescue mission."

Duncan was standing with a dozen or so villagers who looked to be guarding their captured prize as though it might come alive and try to escape. The smugglers' boat was unmarked, with no registration of any kind, no flags, and no transponder. It was a sea ghost, stateless and unidentifiable.

As we approached, Duncan came toward us, a warm smile on his face, relief in his eyes. "You did it again, Laura," he said, and nodded in the direction of the village.

"I didn't do it alone," I said, putting my hand on Saad's shoulder, then pointing my thumb over my shoulder at Lindsay.

Cousin Tobias climbed aboard the smugglers' vessel and stood over the controls. He started the engine and the rotors began churning the water. He gave us the thumbs-up.

"We'd better get moving if we hope to catch her," he said.

"Shall we?" I said to Saad and Lindsay.

"Once was enough for me," Lindsay said. "The action hero thing is your deal, not mine."

"Don't say I never try to include you," I said, smiling.

She put on a serious look and flipped me off.

"That's fair," I said.

Saad stared at me with those brown eyes, conveying a multitude of thoughts and emotions at once. His lips moved to speak, but he just sighed a little, then put his hand on my shoulder and gave it a squeeze.

"You've got no business going after her," Aldo said, as though picking one of Saad's thoughts out of the air.

"If you two are going, and there are no other cops around for a hundred miles, then you'll need backup," I said. "If Brodie and McTavish are injured, you'll need our help. I'll leave the cocaine-stealing entomologist to you."

I turned back to Saad. "If I go, you won't stay behind, will you?"

Maybe it was a trick of the light, or the salt breeze blowing off the ocean, but it looked as though his eyes began to water. "Not a chance," he said.

"Then I'm asking you, one more time, let's do something stupid."

"You don't have to ask," he said, climbing aboard.

"Bloody hell," I heard from behind me as I moved to follow him. Before I could turn, Duncan had taken a running jump over the gunwale and landed beside Saad. "I've missed out on the action the last two times," he said.

Aldo unmoored the boat before hopping aboard, too.

"Laura!" Danny yelled as we pulled away from the dock. "Our insurance won't cover this!"

"I'll pay out of pocket," I called back, waving.

"Be careful," he yelled, or maybe it was something else, his words distorted by the wind and the sound of the engine chopping through the water.

The smugglers' vessel was an old fishing boat with a souped-up engine designed for quick escapes back to international waters. With the empty cargo hold and almost nothing onboard, the boat was deceptively fast. With Cousin Tobias at the helm, we raced toward New Britain. There was no way we'd beat the helicopter there, but we figured we could catch up with Celine and stop her from getting off the island with the cocaine. Everything depended on where the helicopter set them down.

"We can't even be sure where they're going to land," Duncan said. "What I mean is, what's to stop her from hijacking the helicopter and having it drop her closer to her rendezvous point?"

"You could be right," I said. "It depends on how cold-blooded she really is. The smart move would be not to show her hand until the very last minute, creating no alarm, no resistance. That means she'll land at the predetermined coordinates and pretend that everything is normal until she takes off with the drugs."

"And if she's really cold-blooded?" he asked.

"Then she might show her hand the moment they approach the island, taking the chance that either no one will resist, or being prepared to act if they do."

"She'll also have to kill them once she's on the ground, to prevent them from radioing for the authorities," Aldo added.

"Maybe," I said. "But she's more likely to just disable their communications."

"She's killed before," Saad said, just loud enough to be heard over the wind.

We crossed the Dampier Strait, the island of New Britain looming large in the distance. But then something caught my eye and suddenly I was less concerned with what was ahead of us, and more with what was behind me. Tucked into the corner of the bridge was a large black tote with grey handles. I popped it open, revealing an eagle-sized drone and a remote control with a built-in monitor.

"Is that your Ropen?" Duncan asked.

I powered it on and the thing lit up with the same haunting violet glow I saw the other night.

"It looks like it," I said.

"So, the smugglers used this to try to locate their missing drugs?" Saad asked.

"And now we're going to use it for the same purpose," I said.

"What do you have in mind, Laura?" Aldo asked.

We motored around the coast of West New Britain, heading for Cape Gloucester. It was the closest port to where the helicopter was set to land and the most likely spot from which Celine would plan to make her escape. It seemed unlikely that she would try to get to either Akonga or Kandrian, since she would have to go around Langila, an active volcano rising over a kilometre above sea level.

The harbour at Sag Sag, which had been a staging point for Japanese forces during the Second World War, was bustling with activity when we arrived. Dozens of boats were zipping around the harbour, with fishermen bringing their catches ashore. Cousin Tobias arrived at the same conclusion I had: there was no room for us. Instead, he pointed the nose of the craft toward a beach just southeast of the harbour.

"That's where the chopper was headed," Aldo said, pointing over the port side toward a cone-shaped mountain — Langila volcano.

Cousin Tobias gave the engine a rest, letting the tide and our momentum take us closer to the shore. When the bow of the ship wedged into the sand, it stopped us short of the shore by at least twenty feet or so. Cousin Tobias dropped the anchor into the sandy bottom then he and Aldo hopped over the gunwale into the knee-deep water. Aldo reached up and offered me a hand. I gave him the drone.

"This will come in handy," I said.

Saad and Duncan hopped down after me and the five of us splashed toward the beach. A small shore bird flew off as we approached. Aldo checked his GPS, then scanned the hillside, studying the trails that criss-crossed it for the right one to take him to the helicopter.

"I'll cover the harbour," Cousin Tobias said. "If Celine has a boat waiting, it'll be there. One of the locals will know something."

Cousin Tobias ran along the beach toward the harbour.

"Go with him, Duncan," I said. "None of us should be by ourselves."

The moment I said that, I noticed that Aldo had left the drone on the beach and jogged off through the tall grass, and into the trees that bordered it.

"Let's follow him," Saad said, taking a few steps in his direction.

"Let's get the drone in the air first," I said, activating the machine and its controls.

Aldo wasn't hard to follow. Haste tends to leave "loud" traces — deeper footprints, broken stalks of grass, snapped branches. We also knew pretty much where he was going, so it was simple to discern the most likely trail he'd take to get there.

I sent the drone straight up in the air before leaving the beach, making sure it was at a safe height before losing sight of it in the tree cover. Saad led the way, as my attention was focused mostly on the screen atop the drone's controls. The bird's-eye view allowed me to scout the trail ahead of us, then rise above it toward the plateau where the helicopter was supposed to have landed.

We had no way of knowing if the helicopter had even made it, or if Celine had the pilot divert. I assumed that she hadn't. With all that could go wrong, it was better to stick with one set location, since she might not be in constant communication with whoever she was meeting. It was also safer to not give the game away until the very last moment.

Suddenly, the blades of a rotor became visible in black and white on the drone control's screen. Nothing seemed amiss, but there was no activity in the immediate vicinity of the helicopter. I took the drone higher, looking for any movement. At the edge of the frame, I could make out a body stretched out on the limestone. I sent the drone lower. It looked like Dr. McTavish, lying face down.

"Shit!" I said.

He was lying beside a path made up of large stone steps that curved and switched back. I followed the trail with the drone until I confirmed it was the only way down. It also meant that Celine would likely be heading toward us on that same trail. She was probably armed and definitely dangerous, with the added desperation of a person who was cornered. If we heard the sound of gunfire, we'd know Celine had run into Aldo.

When the trail Saad and I was on merged with a wider trail that wound its way up and around the volcano, Saad stopped and grabbed my arm. "Look!" he said, pointing down to a set of fresh tire tracks.

The trail was just wide enough for an ATV to comfortably navigate. So, it was possible that Celine never planned on making her escape through the harbour at Sag Sag at all, but had arranged to take an ATV and disappear deeper into the island, making her damn near impossible to track. If she was on the ATV already, and somehow out of earshot, then she was in the wind. Were it not for the pilot, Brodie, and Dr. McTavish, then we might as well go back to the beach and work on our tans.

We decided to continue up. I sent the drone farther ahead and scanned the trail until Aldo appeared on the screen. I watched as he paused for a moment to examine an ATV that had been concealed beneath some camouflage netting. The trail narrowed and took a steep incline up. Aldo began climbing.

I manoeuvred the drone higher and saw movement farther up the trail. I couldn't zoom in, but it looked to be a person moving downward at a good pace. It became one of those Train A, Train B equations. Celine would be carrying the duffel bag of drugs along with any personal supplies, so she'd be weighted down, but also moving downhill. Aldo, moving uphill, was likely winded from the pace he'd maintained for the last half-hour. Whoever was able to spot the other first was likely the one who would survive. I needed to give Aldo the edge.

It was clear that it was that one time of day for me to be an asshole. As Celine ran toward Aldo and the ATV, I manoeuvred the drone down, buzzing it over her head and missing my target by only a few inches. If I could get her to cry out or fire at the drone, she'd give her position away and tip off Aldo to her presence. I angled the drone toward her again. This time, Celine hit the dirt and reached into her waistband. I steadied the drone and watched as she drew out a small pistol. She popped one round off, but missed her target. She then immediately put her hands up. Aldo had made it to her. Celine tossed her gun off the side of the trail into the forest below and turned around slowly. It was all over so quickly.

We left the drone hovering above as we climbed up after the ex–royal marine. I followed Saad's lead, glancing from the back of his T-shirt to the drone's screen then back again. As we got to the place where they'd been standing, we realized that Celine was gone. Aldo was lying on the ground.

"Check on him," I told Saad. "Celine can't be far."

I began running up the trail toward the helicopter, staying low to the ground. Was Celine still armed? I hadn't even bothered to check whether there was a gun on the ground near Aldo. I looked back at Saad and he gave me the thumbs-up, letting me know Aldo was okay. I moved a bit farther up the trail to a place where the mountainside jutted out, the trail reduced to a narrow ledge around it. With my back against the rock, I inched around it until I saw Celine coming at me like lightning.

Moving carefully with the rock wall as my guide, I kept my eyes on her. Any fight on so narrow a ledge would surely result in one of us going over, and I wasn't going to chance that it might be me. I heard my instructor's voice in my head, reminding me that an attacker can always move forward faster than I could retreat, but I didn't have much choice. I needed to pick my spot.

Celine had a look of cruel determination on her face. I turned away from her for only a second to get safely down to where Saad and Aldo were. When I turned back, I only had enough time to get my arms up and cover my head as she came at me. A kick that high was a gamble and I didn't get a chance to make her pay for it. Celine was equal parts power and grace. I've sparred with a lot of fighters, even some local champs, and only the really good ones can pull off head kicks without losing balance, speed, and power.

As I circled away from her right side, she faked a jab then caught me on the hip with a lead-leg teep. My ass hit the dirt and I rolled back as she came toward me. Before taking another shot at me, Celine turned sharply ninety degrees.

Saad came around, fists up, a look of frightened determination on his face. He fired a jab, which she slipped, and a cross, which she ducked away from. Celine dug a shovel hook into Saad's floating ribs. As he bent over, reeling, she kicked the back of his knee, putting him down. Using her other leg, she sent a roundhouse kick toward the side of his head. He covered up at the last second, seemingly remembering my rule of always shelling up when you couldn't identify what your opponent was doing. The kick knocked him over, but the damage could have been much worse.

Aldo began to stir, looking first at Celine then over toward a patch of tall grass nearby. If Celine didn't finish us all off soon, it would be three against one. I rushed her from behind.

She turned, hands up and ready for me, but not for Saad. He lunged and grabbed her right ankle and clung to it, taking away her footwork. I fired off a teep of my own, kicking her back and using Saad's body to trip her.

Celine hit the grass and kicked free of Saad, driving her heel into his forearm as he blocked and fended her off as best he could. I jumped over his prone body, trying to land on Celine's ankle. She drew it back quickly, getting her legs back under her body and shooting up to her feet. She moved clear of Saad, hands up by her face, fingers curled into fists.

"So, you think you're a tough little bitch, eh?" she hissed, her upper lip curling into a snarl.

"I'm sorry, you sound far too posh for that kind of trash talk," I spat back.

We moved in a parallel orbit, circling away from each other's right side, the power side in the orthodox stance. Adrenalin gave me tunnel vision with Celine at the centre. My movements were choreographed, not a result of decisions I was making, but training stored in my muscles and programmed into my nervous system. She'd make the first move. She had to. I could circle her all day and wait for Aldo and Saad to get up, then she'd be toast.

Celine tried the teep again, which I backed away from, but she followed it up with a jab cross. It was time to do the unexpected. I slipped inside the jab, putting myself in the line of fire for the cross. Shelling up with my left arm, I took the full power of the cross on my bicep. I didn't back off, but shot both arms forward. The blade of my right forearm chopped into the junction of her neck and shoulder, my left hooking under her right arm, holding it close to my body. My right hand gripped the back of her neck and I fired two knees, one into her thigh, the other into her stomach. Once she was doubled over, I pushed down on the back of her neck while lifting her arm up, stepping back and giving myself room to turn her right into the dirt.

Celine hit the ground and launched her Hail Mary without missing a beat, kicking me in the side of the head. It wasn't a powerful blow, from the side it must have looked like something from a Jane Fonda work-out VHS, but it caught me by surprise. It was enough to break my grip. Celine rolled free and was up to her feet again.

"You fight dirty," she said.

"I'm sorry, are there rules I'm supposed to be following out here?"

"I suppose not," she said, rushing forward.

I sidestepped, then circled around her. "There's the posh Celine I know and don't like," I said.

She turned toward me and swung her left arm like a baseball bat. I swayed back and let her fist pass me before catching her with a cross, staggering her. I pressed my advantage, throwing a left before realizing that she was baiting me. Before I knew it, she had her hands clasped around the back of my head, pulling me down into a double plum clinch. I put my forearms across my body as she began rifling knee shots in.

"Laura?" Saad yelled as he got back to his feet.

"Get this bitch off me!" I screamed.

Saad came around behind her, grabbing her by the shoulders, which I would have told him was a bad idea were I not struggling to avoid having my insides tenderized. Celine pushed off me, launching herself into Saad, elbowing him in ribs, trying to hit the same spot as before. She achieved the desired response, then turned and caught him with a left hook that sent him down again.

I lunged low, firing a cross right into her liver. She staggered, trying to turn with her arms up in a shell, but I came over the top with an elbow, cutting the delicate skin of her forehead. As she reeled, I switched to low-line targets — a lead roundhouse kick to her rear thigh before stepping off-line and hitting the same leg with a right roundhouse.

Aldo, from his hands and knees, jumped up and charged toward Celine, scooping her up from behind like a pro wrestler attempting a back-arch suplex. He turned her and dumped her down hard on the ground.

"All right, you little tart," he said, "enough is enough."

From the ground she fired a kick into Aldo's knee. He stumbled back while Celine scrambled for the patch of grass.

"Shouldn't have called her a tart," I said, scrambling around the big man.

Celine reached into a particular spot of grass and withdrew Busby's pistol. There was no getting to her in time. If she turned around now, she'd do so shooting. I dropped to one knee and pulled the flare gun from my pocket, pointed it, and pulled the trigger. The flare made a crackling, spitting sound as it left the barrel. It flew like a shooting star, straight toward Celine's loose hair, which whirled around her head as she spun. Her gun went off as the flare caught the side of her head. We both cried out and Zach's words echoed in my head: *A gunshot wound is a death sentence out here.*

Saad took his shirt off, pressing it against my new-found shoulder hole as the blue-grey fabric turned an ugly charcoal shade. Aldo ran toward Celine, who was cradling her face. He yanked her gun hand away from her face, removing the pistol from it and revealing the flare's damage. She didn't have a model's face anymore. He tried pulling her up, but she fought like a wolf in a snare. The power, agility, and technique were gone, replaced by pure feral instinct. She managed to break free and staggered backward.

"Celine!" Aldo said a half-second before she fell back down the steep incline.

I tried to get up but Saad held me in place.

"Stay still, you've been shot."

"No shit," I said.

Saad chuckled, then I chuckled. I full on laughed. It was a weird cocktail of chemicals in my brain behind the laughter, but that didn't matter. Aldo stared over the edge for a few moments then came over to me.

"Can you see her?" I asked.

"She's rolled into the trees," he said. "If she survived the fall, I don't envy her."

"Can we get down there?"

"Laura, you're more stubborn than a terrier."

"I'm a dog person, so that doesn't offend me."

"We need to get you to the helicopter. There's a first aid kit."

Aldo took off his belt and looped it around my arm, drawing it tight into my armpit, cutting off the flow of blood to the wound just above where the deltoid met the biceps. "Saad, when I say go, remove your shirt from the wound. Laura, you're not going to enjoy this."

"I stopped having fun the moment I almost got bit by that snake," I said.

"Go!" he said.

Aldo drew the belt tight over my shoulder, cutting off the blood flow to my arm. Saad applied his shirt again and both men helped me to my feet.

"Luckily it's just a flesh wound," Aldo said.

There was a temptation to say "I don't feel lucky," but out of respect to Busby, I kept quiet. The helicopter wasn't far, and I would soon be bandaged and hopefully in a hospital not long after.

SEVENTEEN

If pterosaurs were still living, we would expect to find some kind of fossil evidence that they persisted much longer than previously thought.

— Riley Black, "Don't Get Strung Along by the 'Ropen' Myth," *Smithsonian*, August 16, 2010

I AWOKE IN A SMALL HOSPITAL ROOM THAT resembled an asylum from an old movie. I'm so used to large hospital rooms with pastel walls and crash kits and all sorts of other gizmos that old-style hospitals look more like prisons. Saad was sitting in a chair wedged between the bed and the cinder block wall that had a thick coat of white paint. He had his computer open on his lap.

"Have you eaten anything?" I found myself asking.

"I had a banana," he said.

"That's it?"

"I haven't got much of an appetite."

"How long have you been here?"

"Since they brought you in," he said.

"You don't need to watch over me."

"Yes, I do," he said matter-of-factly, his eyes drifting back to his computer screen.

"What are you doing?" I asked, nodding toward the computer.

"Did you see that mark on Celine? The ovular shape on her side?"

"I was pretty busy getting my ass kicked," I said, "but yeah, I caught a glimpse. It looked like some kind of brand."

He turned the computer toward me so I could get a good view of the screen. "Do you think it looked like this?"

On the screen was an Egyptian-style cartouche, but where you might expect to see the sun in the top half of the oval, there was a spoked wheel. In the bottom half, instead of an ankh there was a cross. I closed my eyes and tried to picture the mark on Celine's skin. It hit me then that it was about the size of a quarter, the same size as the scar tissue on Zach's neck, like he once carried the same brand, then had it removed.

"That's about the right shape," I said, "but I can't confirm there was that much detail in what I saw."

"I saw it better than you did," he said. "On account of her manhandling me like I was a child."

"She rag-dolled all of us, Aldo included. There's no shame in that."

I believed what I said, but that didn't stop the current of anger humming through my nervous system that told me how badly I wanted a rematch.

"What's that symbol?" I asked.

"It's the symbol for the Legion de Cartouche, an organization founded by a man who called himself Cartouche, in France, during La Regence. He was a famous highwayman who stole from the rich and gave to the poor."

"So, a French Robin Hood?"

"Apparently. Until the authorities caught him and executed him on a Catherine wheel. His death inspired a following, almost like a quasi-religious cult, a society of thieves. For the next three hundred years, this group was highwaymen, pirates, con men, outlaws, but always stealing from the rich."

"But not always giving to the poor?"

"There's talk that they procure food and vaccines for poor people and refugees. But some online rumours make them out to be more like anarchists, stealing from royalty, organized crime, corrupt officials, people in power basically."

"Is there any conclusive proof that they're real? Or is this all just internet hearsay, like claims the Knights Templar are still around, bankrolled by fortunes their forebears robbed from the Middle East during the Crusades?"

"We saw the symbol," he said, raising his eyebrows.

"That doesn't mean there's an international guild of thieves operating from the shadows," I scoffed. "It just means that someone took inspiration from something they found online."

"But think about it. Zach wanted to buy his way back into some group. This could be the group."

Someone knocked rhythmically on the door. The knob turned and Cousin Tobias walked in with a woman in her midforties. She had strawberry-blond hair and was wearing a tan pantsuit and leather pumps with a thick heel.

"Hello, hello," Cousin Tobias said before sidestepping and presenting the woman to us as though she were a guest of honour. "This is Federal Agent Sonja Campbell. She was overseeing Agent Busby's side of the operation. She flew in from headquarters in Canberra."

"How do you do?" she said, broadcasting her words to both of us as if not really expecting an answer. "We'll need a report from both of you before you leave."

"I'm sorry about Agent Busby," I said. "I was with him at the end. I wish I could have done more."

She looked at her shoes for a split second then back to me. "Yes, well, from the sounds of things, you did far more than your share."

It wasn't the "attagirl" I would have liked. Campbell almost sounded annoyed, as though I should have minded my own business. But I suppose being a Monday-morning quarterback is part and parcel of a bureaucrat's job. They have rules and regulations and no room for anything else.

"Without Laura, the drugs might not have been recovered, the missing boys might not have been found, and more people might have been hurt," Cousin Tobias said.

"Believe it or not, I don't go looking for trouble," I said, "and I try not to interfere when there's a choice."

"No, the sergeant is right, we may not have accomplished anything were it not for your heroism, and that of Mr. Javed here, and Mr. Middleton."

"Did you hear that, Saad? 'Heroism.'"

Saad smiled. Maybe it was the pain meds, or just the overwhelming relief of being out of danger, but I no longer felt anchored to the seriousness of the situation. We had made it.

"But understand this, from an operational standpoint, this is a failure. We lost an agent. It was too high a price to pay for the arrest of a trafficker at the bottom of the food chain and the recovery of some duffel bags full of cocaine, regardless of its street value."

"I get that," I said.

Saad closed his eyes and nodded. Cousin Tobias lowered his gaze.

"Has Zach given up anything useful?" I asked.

"I doubt very much he has anything useful to give," Agent Campbell said. "He and his cronies were just thieves. We'll get him on conspiracy to commit murder in the death of Adam Tarver, but that's a matter for the local police."

"He hasn't given up Celine Yi?" I asked.

"Celine Yi is not Celine Yi," Cousin Tobias said.

"How do you mean?" Saad asked.

"The British police have managed to find Celine Yi in Shotley Bridge Hospital in the north of England. She was registered as a Jane Doe," Agent Campbell said.

"Is she all right?" I asked.

"They think she'll make a full recovery," Cousin Tobias said. "Apparently she was given a drug that put her into a coma. She had no ID and no way to establish her identity while she was unconscious."

"That's incredible," Saad said.

"The police have found email correspondence on Celine's computer from a woman claiming to be a journalist who wanted to interview her before she left for the expedition," Cousin Tobias said. "Celine had shared her research, even personal details, with the 'journalist,' not realizing she was giving away her identity. The last time her roommate saw her was when she was leaving for the interview. That didn't seem too strange at the time, as Celine had a very early flight to catch at Heathrow before flying to PNG. Apparently, no such journalist exists, though the publication she claimed to represent was real enough and she somehow had access to their server."

Agent Campbell took a deep breath, her hands smoothing the front of her jacket. I noticed her nails were neatly manicured with a nice matte finish. They disappeared under the hem of her jacket as she tugged on the fabric.

"Well," she said finally. "I should be off. Thank you again."

A million thoughts seemed to be wrestling for supremacy in her head as she turned and walked toward the door. She seemed to have lost some of her presence. We all watched her leave.

"She is upset because she lost an agent," Cousin Tobias said, looking back at me. "She is not convinced that Agent Busby will have justice."

"I've never seen a more clear-cut case of poetic justice," I said. "The man who shot Busby, who caused him to bleed to death, was shot and bled to death himself only a few feet from where Busby died. What more could she want?"

"Laura, when we returned to the research station, we found no remains."

"What? He died a few feet from the station, in the middle of the clearing. We put a sheet over him," I said.

"That's right," Saad agreed.

"I believe you," Cousin Tobias said. "But it wasn't there when we went to investigate. That white sheet was found caught on some branches, high in a tree halfway up the mountain."

Cousin Tobias made his way toward the door. "I'll let you get some rest," he said. "I'll see you both later."

When he closed the door, his outline was visible through the frosted glass. He seemed to hover there for a few seconds before walking down the hall.

"How is that possible?" I asked.

"What did that elder say about the Ropen and open graves?"

"Don't even start with that," I said, rolling my eyes.

Saad smiled.

"You know, my mom thinks you're a bad influence," Saad said.

"Because I'm always getting us in trouble and/or sent to the hospital?"

He smiled again, wider this time.

"She might be on to something," I said.

"Maybe we should take a break. From the dangerous stuff, I mean. I'd certainly help find your dad, though, if you wanted help …"

"I don't think I could handle it without you," I said. "But I have to be honest, right now, I'd rather find whoever was impersonating Celine Yi."

"Because she shot you?"

"For a dozen reasons at least," I said. "But, yes, shooting me is somewhere near the top."

Saad just stared at me. I looked away, toward the door, then the crack between it and the floor, shadows of feet passing in the hall. I started to wonder if Saad was starting to get tired of the risks I took.

"Danny thinks we have enough footage to cut an episode together," he said. "Although he thinks we'll have to double down on the creationism versus evolution debate. He assured me that you and I wouldn't be necessary, as it would just mean shooting interviews with Duncan and Joshua as they discussed pterosaur morphology, the prehistoric survivor paradigm, and the age of the earth."

"Great," I said. "I get shot and Danny gets to 'teach the controversy.'"

"On the bright side, the show gets to go on."

It didn't occur to me until then that that whole misadventure could have cost me the show.

"I'm having a hard time seeing what's next for us," I said.

"I'm going home," Saad said.

"That is the plan," I said.

"No, *home* home," he said. "I'm going to Karachi. We're so much closer here than when we're in the U.S., and … well, we almost died. Again. I just want to see my mom, my sister and her kids."

"I understand."

"Come with me," he said.

"Really?"

Just then my phone dinged. It was an email notification. Thank god for Wi-Fi. I glanced at the phone out of habit but was fully prepared to ignore it. But it was my PI. The subject line: "What do you think?" I saw the little paperclip icon that meant he'd sent an attachment. When I opened it, it contained a photo of a man in about his sixties, with long hair tied in a ponytail and a beard like a lumberjack. The photo looked recent. The email contained one line.

"Is this your father?"

ACKNOWLEDGEMENTS

I'M GRATEFUL FOR THE SUPPORT OF MY agent, Kelvin Kong, as well as Scott Fraser and the entire Dundurn Press team. This book in particular owes a debt to Eduard Habsburg, whose advice influenced certain plot points. The story itself would not have been possible without the research of Jonathan D. Whitcomb, Darren Naish, David Martill, and David Woetzel. With all my work, I rely heavily on the safety net of friends who I bounce ideas off of, or at least discuss topics like cryptozoology with at length. Many thanks to Marc "Pops" Medwid, Pete Hamilton, Bryan Ibeas, Mandy Hopkins, and Neil Springer. Huge thanks to Vivian Lin, for all the support she has given to the Creature X books. Lastly, and most importantly, my heartfelt thanks to my partner, Sheeza Sarfraz, who never quits and never lets me do so, either.

ABOUT THE AUTHOR

 J.J. Dupuis writes fiction, poetry, and satire. His work has been published in magazines and journals such as *Valve*, *Foliate Oak*, *Spadina Literary Review*, and *University of Toronto Magazine*. J.J. is the founding editor of the *Quarantine Review*, a literary journal born out of self-isolation. He lives and works in East York, Toronto, and is an avid outdoorsman and martial artist.